THE FALLING

Published by Snowy Wings Publishing.
snowywingspublishing.com

ISBN: 978-1-946202-33-8

Interior formatting by Key of Heart Designs.
Interior graphics by Vectorian.
Cover design by Gabrielle Prendergast.

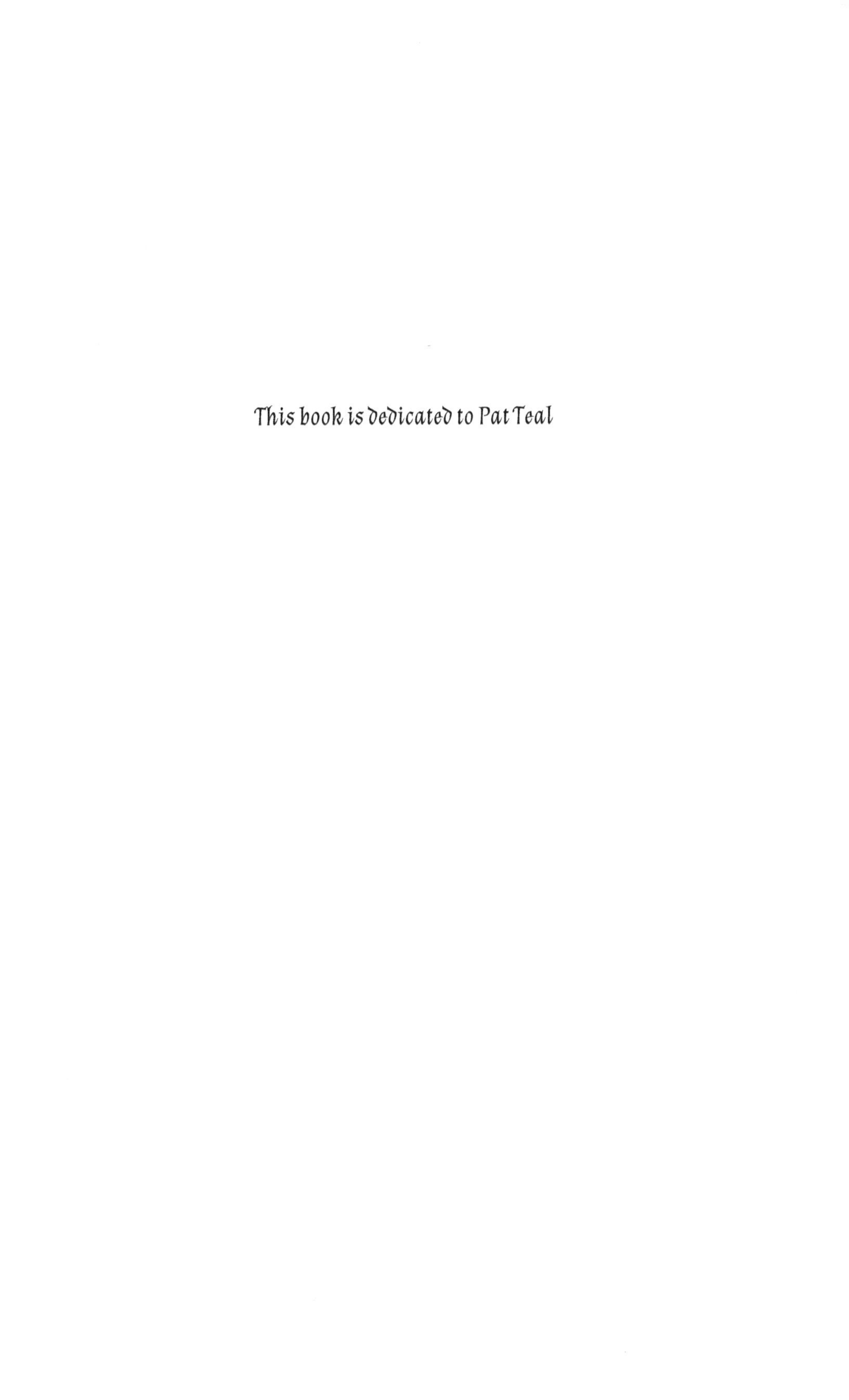

This book is dedicated to Pat Teal

Prologue

A Forest's life is beyond what the normal, everyday eye can see. In fact, the regular goings-on of a particularly enchanted Forest are completely lost on a typical human's perception. But the energies of these Forests can be felt by all who stumble into them, whether by mistake or for a purpose.

These energies stem from the Higher Spirits of the Forests, whose life-giving light provides the harmony necessary for the Forests to exist. The animals and the beings maintain this harmony with the direction, protection, guidance, and love from the Higher Spirits. The Forest featured in this particular story is watched over by four Higher Spirits:

Sator, who directs,

Labete, who protects,

Arepo, who guides,

And The Yew, the Highest Spirit, who loves.

These spirits of light are counterbalanced by four Under Spirits, who provide the order necessary for the Forest to remain harmonious. These

Under Spirits are the paradox of the Higher Spirits:

Doppel, who deceives,

Agrimon, who destroys,

Valerian, who follows,

And Gorgon, the Undermost Spirit, who provides chaos.

And while love reigned supreme in all the kingdoms of the Forest, a centuries-old rivalry between the Yew and Gorgon had not been forgotten by the passing of time and years of harmony and balance. Gorgon swore that one day he would enact revenge upon the Highest Spirit who cast him into the underworld so many generations ago.

An opportunity for Gorgon was presented one day, as the Nymph Kingdom was in dire need of the appointment of a new Nymph King. The Higher Spirits met with the Under Spirits to decide who would be the next king, yet Agrimon was sent with an agenda from Gorgon, who sought triumph over the Yew. The Undermost Spirit had instructed Agrimon to possess his counterpart, Labete, and influence him to select Alston, an affluent yet ignorant nymph to become the next Nymph King. Alston was to apprentice under the protection of Labete.

The Higher Spirits strongly disagreed with Labete's decision and felt as though Labete had, in a way, betrayed the Yew. And when Labete tried to return to his rightful place as a Higher Spirit after the apprenticeship, the other Higher Spirits refused him and instead cast him into the Forest to live among the mortals.

Labete was hurt, infuriated, and bitter, feelings unbeknownst to him prior to existing in a mortal realm. He became more and more vulnerable to Agrimon's influence, and eventually experienced a complete fall from grace. This fall created enough chaos necessary for Gorgon to rise from the underworld for the sole purpose of casting the Yew into Lapis Mountain, then was forced to return to the underworld to bask in the chaos that he created. To this day, the Yew remains entrapped in Lapis Mountain, in a deep slumber, until a being of the Forest prompts him awake with a magical spell. And thus, the falling in the Forest began.

But before our story can truly begin, one must verse oneself in the nature of what the story is about. Forest nymphs. But what is a Forest nymph? Well to understand what they are one must also understand what they are not. Nymphs are not faeries. They are not gnomes, and they are not trolls. If one had to physically describe a nymph, it would be a small likeness of a human, similar in appearance to a faery, but lacking the wings. If one had to compare a nymph to any mythical creature, it would probably be a leprechaun, though the story does not take place in Ireland, but rather the Pacific Northwest of North America. Nymphs are far more streamlined than leprechauns, as well as they have little interest in gold or rainbows, or even growing an overly large beard. There is no real term for these types of nymphs, but if on the islands of Hawaii they would refer to these small beings as "menehune." On the islands, however, the menehune are notoriously mischievous, and frequently play tricks on humans. Forest nymphs haven't an appetite for such shenanigans. They prefer to go about their business, living their lives as hardworking beings, whether it be by way of farmer, seamstress, blacksmith, tradesman, or warrior. Those who find themselves down the path to becoming a warrior find quite an arduous life ahead of them, though the position is extremely desired.

And though the life of a warrior is romanticized in this time of nymphs, there was once a time when there was no need for warriors of any species. In the earlier times, every species lived in harmony. Even humans had not yet found their thirst for greed and resources, nor the need to manipulate the environment around them. And though the Native Americans maintained a respect for all beings co-habituating the forests, the arrival of settlers prompted the disconnect between humans, nature, and the "mythical" beings. This disconnect grew larger with each tree that was cut without replanting another, and every residence that was erected on sacred land created from the very fabric of the spirits that the settlers disrespected. What were now always considered to be inhabiting the forests became "mythical", and sightings of the small forest dwellers waned over time. This was due to the fact that the very spiritual beings of the forest began to resent and fear the humans, and with this fear and strong negative emotions came a whirlwind of dark energy that began to engulf the forests from the consecrated burial grounds of the angered ancestors. This is theorized to be the beginning of what will now be known as "The Falling".

The Falling

The Forest Spirit Series, Book One

T. Damon

CHAPTER 1

"**N**arena! You are going to get us in trouble again!" Nyxen, a dark-haired, strong-browed nymph frantically called to his older sister, who was dashing ahead of him through the Forest. He struggled to keep up as his athletic sister sprinted toward the outskirts of Nymph Kingdom. "Seriously, Narena! You know I can't run as fast as you!" Nyxen wailed.

He followed his sister through a maze of twisted oak trees, darted around towering redwoods, and delicately hopped from pebble to pebble over the Forest's creek.

"Hey, who asked you to come with me?" Narena called back over her shoulder.

"What...choice...do...I...have?" Nyxen panted, catching up as she came to a stop at the bottom of an old oak tree. "I'm the one who has to report." He brushed a trail of sweat off his brow and scowled in his sister's direction.

"Honestly, Nyxen, I really don't care. Report what you want. Meanwhile, this is my life to enjoy and no one is going to stop me, certainly not you or your neurotic rules."

Narena scaled the tree. Nyxen gasped every time she almost missed her footing, unable to tear his eyes away from his sister. He did not feel comfortable enough with his own athletic ability to follow his sister to such extreme heights, but he was not about to let her out of his sight, even for one second. When Narena finally reached a crooked branch high in the Forest's canopy, she looked down and stuck her tongue out at her brother. In the far off distance, the towering form of Lapis Mountain stood proudly atop a cluster of trees, providing a breathtaking sight for the adolescent nymph.

From a young age, Nyxen had a tendency to be overprotective of his sister, and tried his best to look out for her despite her mischievous ways. It almost seemed as though he were the elder sibling, and she the younger. But Nyxen lacked the carefree outlook Narena prided herself on, though she did admire his neurotic nature when it proved useful. And since it was no longer acceptable to gallivant through certain areas of the Forest, he had major right to be so careful on this day.

"Narena. I know what you're doing, and you know the king has forbidden it. No one is supposed to watch the warriors' morning drill. What if someone sees you?" Nyxen hissed upward, but found his sister simply ignored him in response.

"Will you calm down little brother?" she finally replied after some time, not bothering to tear her eyes away from scanning the tree line ahead of her. "I've almost gotten close enough to see them. You worry too much, the Forest won't betray me."

"Narena...!" Nyxen hissed, this time sounding more irritated than he had before. "If you are not out of that tree by the time I count to three..."

"You'll what?" Narena hissed back, annoyed that he would even consider giving her such an ultimatum. "String me up by my toes?" She giggled. "Shh! Be quiet for a moment... I think I see something."

Nyxen folded his arms and stared helplessly up the tree, but Narena's attention was now drawn to the three male nymphs crouched near the sacred clearing not far from her perch. She recognized all of them—but they certainly weren't doing morning drill.

What are they doing?

She could not hear what General Felide was saying to his son, Kellen, but she could tell the younger nymph looked fairly irritated. And that Rowan, King Alston's warrior son, was ignoring them both, running his bony fingers through his thick, golden hair as he normally did.

"What's going on?!" Nyxen called upward.

"SHH!" Narena replied, hunching even lower. Nyxen sighed and sat himself at the base of the tree, leaning his back to the trunk before closing his eyes. But Narena of course did not notice what her brother was doing, as she was solely focused on whatever it was the three male nymphs seemed to be waiting for.

After several minutes, a small, mousey creature crept out from the brush toward the three warriors. Felide immediately moved toward it, spoke for a few minutes, then turned back to the other nymphs.

Whatever he was saying got cut short by a bloodcurdling shriek as a swarm of hymenopteral insects appeared out of nowhere, engulfed the creature's body, and then quickly buzzed toward the other nymphs. Narena slapped her hand across her mouth to keep from screaming at the sight of what they'd left behind: a blinding white skeleton.

"Run!" Narena heard Felide shriek. "Back to the palace!"

Chapter 2

ap, rap, rap.

Narena filtered into consciousness, then turned over and drifted away.

Rap, rap, rap.

What in the world is that noise?

Rap, rap, rap.

"Narena!" Nyxen's voice pierced into Narena's mind. She grumbled, turned over again and thrust her pillow over her head. "Narena!" Nyxen's voice again.

"What?" Narena finally replied, but remained in her bed.

"You have some guests at the door."

"Tell them I'm busy," Narena replied, annoyed.

"For the love of the Yew, Narena, just come to the door."

"Oh, all right." Narena reluctantly got up and made her way toward the door to her bedroom. On the way, she caught a glimpse of her short, disheveled dark brown hair, which was standing upright in all directions of her head, awkwardly framing her cute, button nose. Her deep orange eyes peered back at her, and she sighed as she sauntered to the front entryway to her home, which was located between the protruding roots of an old oak tree. "Okay, what do you want?" She was not in a mood to even attempt to hide any form of disdain for her brother, or whoever it was at the door who dared interrupt her rest. Especially after what she had been through recently.

But rather than the door to door fox-bristle broom salesman she was expecting, standing at the front door was a lumpy salamander, its skin glistening with mucous, black as night with a rusty chestnut brown stripe swooping from head to tail. "Hi Narena," he said. "It's certainly been a while, hasn't it?"

"Hawthorne! What are you doing here? I haven't seen you since I lived at the palace. How did you know where I live now?" Narena replied, rushing to her old friend for a much overdue embrace.

"I knocked on a few doors and this guy said he would show me the way."

"What guy?"

"Um, hello Narena," a deep voice stammered from behind Hawthorne.

Narena peeked around her salamander friend to find Kellen, and her eyes widened. His sun-kissed skin glimmered in the light that shone through the doorway, reflecting even the smallest beam of sunlight on the napes of his muscular frame. Narena couldn't help but catch a glance at his deep green eyes, and without realizing it, blushed.

Kellen was quite a few years older than Narena, though maintained an air about himself that made him seem much younger. But though his handsome face was youthful, he possessed a sense of authority along with his take-control attitude. Each muscle, though tattooed with battle scars, was effortlessly perfect and delicately placed to ripple and gleam with each movement. Kellen had always been admired by female and male nymphs alike, as his handsomeness often coincided with his rebellious attitude in social situations. But this was a meeting under a different circumstance, certainly no party or gathering at the Holly Bush Pub.

"What are you doing here?" Narena asked. "I'm so glad you're all right!" she added before she could stop herself. She felt her face flush again despite her best efforts. Kellen looked a bit confused, but kept a slight smile on the corners of his mouth.

"All right? Why wouldn't he be all right?" Nyxen interrupted. "What's going on? Does this have anything to do with what you saw yesterday, Narena?"

"Shush, Nyxen!"

"What is he talking about?" Kellen demanded.

"Nothing, nothing. I wasn't there, I didn't see anything." Kellen's eyes narrowed.

"You weren't *where*? *What* didn't you see? Come on—spill it!"

"I don't have to tell you anything," she muttered through clenched teeth.

"She won't even tell me!" Nyxen interjected, "but she's been hiding in her room ever since."

"I needed a decent rest. I've had a rough last few days."

"Not until yesterday..." Nyxen trailed off. "Before that you seemed fine."

"Define 'fine' for Narena," Kellen chuckled. "Is 'fine' participating in her usual oddball antics or not? Refresh my memory."

"I ought to refresh your face with a knuckle sandwich," Narena grunted.

"Did something scare you yesterday, Narena?" Hawthorne asked. "Because to me you seem a little off as well. Did you see something horrible and frightening and you can't get rid of the image out of your mind?"

Narena stopped. She took her friend's squishy hand. "Did that happen to you, Hawthorne? What did you see?"

Hawthorne shook his head. "I can't say it... out loud. I... I... just can't say it. It was too... horrible. So horrible!"

"Horrible, like... a bright white skeleton where there used to be somebody?" Narena whispered.

"How did you know?" Hawthorne whispered back.

"Hey, how much did you see?" Kellen demanded again.

"I only saw the skeletons," Hawthorne said. "Dozens and dozens of skeletons."

"What about you?" Kellen said, taking Narena's arm. "What, exactly, did *you* see?"

"Yes!" Nyxen said, almost shouting. "Tell us already, for love of the Yew!"

Narena's eyes teared up. "I saw it all," she said softly. "I saw the little mousey creature. I saw the swarm—some kind of insects I've never seen before. They can't, they couldn't be a part of our Forest! And I saw them..." A tear dropped from her orange eyes. "They... they..."

"They what?!" Nyxen cried. "What did they do?"

"They ate the creature," Kellen finished for Narena. "They swarmed him and ate every morsel of him, until nothing was left but his bones."

Nyxen gasped, and Hawthorne began to cry softly. Narena wiped her face and set her jaw. She was, after all, her father's daughter.

"That's terrible!" Nyxen cried. "Who are these insects? How did they even get into our Forest? What's the king doing about this?"

"The king is taking it under advisement," Kellen said in the tone of a court spokesman. "The king advises his subjects to take care when out in the Forest."

"What in the world does that mean?!" Narena demanded.

"Nothing," Kellen admitted. "It means nothing. It means the king has no idea what to do."

"So it's up to us, isn't it?"

"No, it's up to us warriors. There's nothing *you* can do. You're just a research scientist. You talk to birds and squirrels. This is out of your league."

Narena sighed. Kellen was right. She was, after all, just a research scientist, appointed by King Alston himself to give her some legitimacy in the kingdom with a purpose, a job. Narena, however, was certainly savvy to the real reason she was given her title—a feeble attempt to keep her out of trouble. But despite this, she had always harbored a bitterness from the constant rain of suggestions of how to exist. She felt as though nothing she did was ever good enough, no matter how intelligent it was, simply because someone else, mostly male nymphs, felt threatened by something she did or thought out better than them.

Her mind raced back to a time of being ousted from a bird-watching club because she befriended the birds enough to bring them to meet the members, only to be greeted by fear and anger that she had let her guard down to a creature so much larger than a nymph. After that incident, she had resolved herself to thinking that she could not alter the way others felt about her, only that she could continue to only project her true self to everyone. And if they still rejected it, then she didn't need them.

"Really?" she snapped back at Kellen. "So why are you here instead of out with your unit, beating the bushes to find and destroy these insects?"

"Yeah, why were you home when I knocked?" Hawthorne demanded. "Why weren't you out on maneuvers? Why weren't you out avenging my species' genocide?!"

"Good question," Nyxen joined in. "Very good question. Why are you here instead of out there?" He joined his sister and Hawthorne in looming closer to Kellen, backing him up against the wall by the front door.

Kellen looked slightly nervous, then motioned everyone closer, and the four huddled up.

"I don't really know what's going on," he said quietly. "But I overheard part of the argument between my father and the king. My father wants us to go to war but the king forbade it. He says it's too dangerous. I think he said—I'm not sure, because my father was yelling, and the king was speaking very low—I *think* he said he needs to communicate with..." Kellen looked around before continuing. "Labete," he finished in a whisper.

The three gasped.

CHAPTER 3

"Labete?" Narena asked quietly. "What does Labete have to do with this? He's supposed to protect us! If anything, I'd think that one of the Under Spirits would be behind something like this, not a Higher Spirit."

"I told you, I don't know everything that was said," Kellen replied. "And don't you dare tell a soul of this."

"Who would I tell?" Narena shot back. "The one nymph I might even consider spilling your precious secrets to is standing right beside me."

"Well, you seem to enjoy gallivanting about with every known species in the Forest, how am I to know?"

Narena groaned. "Oh *puh-lease!* Could you be any more jealous?" The two stood almost nose to nose, eyes squinted and brows furrowed at one another.

"Stop it you two," Nyxen interjected. "You're being ridiculous. And something serious is obviously going on here. This bickering is unnecessary. Right, Hawthorne?"

"Absolutely. And as for this whole Labete situation, I am beyond stunned. My sight points to the truth, but I just can't believe that Labete would do something like this to the salamanders," Hawthorne spoke up. "We've always been friends of Labete. We make offerings to the Spirits on a regular basis."

"I can't believe any Higher Spirit would do any kind of thing you've described," Nyxen agreed, as he gently pulled his sister's shoulders backwards and away from her intimidating stance at Kellen's front.

"I don't know," Kellen said. "I can only report what I've overheard, and even that's not much. But I do know this. My father says Labete has changed a great deal since Alston became king, and I don't think the other Higher Spirits were happy that Labete chose him."

"But why would he choose somebody that no one else wanted?" Narena asked. "That doesn't even make sense, not even for one of the Spirits."

Hawthorne gasped. "How can you speak like that of the Higher Spirits?"

Narena shrugged. "We've become accustomed to thinking of them as above us, but they weren't always. They started out just like us, and evolved just like everything else in nature."

"That's blasphemy!" Hawthorne cried, slapping a slimy hand up to his mouth. This was warranted, as he descended from the longest ancestry of sage salamanders—wise elementals containing meditative and intuitive abilities. But very short-lived, as an average salamander's life expectancy didn't often span longer than a decade. All of Hawthorne's ancestors had really made their magical mark on their species, and Hawthorne's desire to honor them was readily apparent in his everyday existence, especially now. He himself was blessed with an innate gift of seer sight, an ability to inherently know truths, much like a form of clairvoyance, but the recent massacre of his entire species seemed to have upset his abilities, as he was finding it more and more difficult to see in the manner he was accustomed.

"No it's not," Nyxen said. "We read all about it in the books the king has in his library, or at least Narena did," he added, "and I listened when she talked about them."

"I don't think your reading has done you any good, Narena," Kellen said. "Unless you read something about how to stop these insects."

"I didn't say I could stop anything. I didn't even say Labete is behind them. I just said the Higher Spirits used to be just like us. So maybe parts of them are still like us," she continued, her brow furrowing with thought.

"What do you mean?" Hawthorne asked.

Narena's voice got very low. "Maybe Labete purposely chose a king the others didn't like."

The four companions looked at each other in shock. No one knew what that could possibly mean. But all knew that the nature of the conversation was growing far too intense for their little bodies to handle at the moment, so collectively decided to take a break and sit down for a bit.

The group wandered into Narena and Nyxen's living room. Narena and Hawthorne sat down together on the pine-green couch and caught up on recent events. Kellen perched himself on the arm of a rusty-colored sitting chair, gazing around at the siblings' various trinkets, feathers, and polished rocks that decorated the room.

"Oh, my head!" Nyxen groaned suddenly, before he was able to sit down. He grabbed his temples and bent over in pain as electricity flashed up his spine, across his forehead, and into his eye sockets.

"What's the matter with him?" Kellen asked, his attention torn away from Narena's collection of oddities.

"He'll be all right," Narena replied, rushing to her brother's side. "He's just getting one of his headaches. He's gotten them his whole life, but it's not something that we announce to the whole Forest, like you probably think we do, Kellen. That's probably why you've never noticed it."

"Looks pretty intense," Kellen said, ignoring her snide remark.

"Yeah, they can really take him out of commission. I'll go put on a pot of herbal tea for him. That usually does the trick." Narena disappeared into the kitchen, and the others trailed behind her to help, leaving Nyxen alone in the foyer.

"Who *are* you?!" Nyxen groaned under his breath at the barely audible voice that had plagued his mind ever since he could remember. "What do you want from me?! I hear you talking, but I can't make out what you're saying, and you're hurting me! Stop it! No, don't get louder! I can't understand you! Stop!"

Helllp uuus. Saaaavvve uusss. The voice grew louder than he recalled ever hearing it.

Nyxen's copper eyes popped wide open, and his heart started pounding. "Who said that?" he whispered aloud. "Who are you? Where are you? What can I do? Who *are you*?!"

Soooon of Giiiniiia. Saaave uusss.

In an instant, the electricity stopped and Nyxen crashed to the floor. "Narena!" he choked out before losing consciousness.

The others trooped back into the foyer. "Nyxen!" Narena cried, rushing to her brother's side and scooping him into her arms. "Nyxen! What happened?"

Nyxen opened his eyes. "It's the Forest, Narena. The Forest talks to me."

"Yeah, right," Kellen said, rolling his eyes. "You're as nutty as your mother!"

Nyxen shook himself out of Narena's grasp, and jumped to his feet. "Careful what you say about my mother, you blood-spiller, you!"

"But he's right," Hawthorne spoke up. "My father used to tell me. He married your parents, you know," he said, grinning to Narena.

"I know, I remember my father telling me. So what?"

"So your mother talked to the trees, that's what. Didn't you know? Everyone else did. All us salamanders, at least," Hawthorne admitted.

"My mother talked to the trees?" Narena said. "Excuse me?"

"Of course!" Nyxen put in excitedly. "That's what they were trying to tell me! That's why they called me 'son of Ginia'!"

"Who called you that?"

"The trees!"

"The trees? Your whole family is nuts," Kellen said with disgust. "I always knew you were all weird. Even back when we were kids. Nerdy Nyxen and Naughty Narena."

"No, we're not weird," Nyxen declared. "Well, not me anyway. And I *did* hear the trees!"

"Ok, Nyx," Narena said, putting her arm around her little brother. "Let's say you heard the trees swaying, and it sounded like words."

"No! I heard the words! For the first time in my life, I heard them clearly!"

"I believe you," his sister said, but he could tell she really didn't. He looked at the others' faces. No one believed him. But he knew what he'd heard, and that was enough for him. And he couldn't expect his sister to believe that a voice accompanied his headaches, for he had never told her.

"I could use some of that tea, sis," he said, making for the kitchen.

Everyone sat at the table, and Narena poured out. "Okay," she said. "Let's start over, now that we've had a chance to regroup. What do we really know about all this Labete stuff?"

"We know a swarm of insects wiped out my species," Hawthorne said.

"We know a swarm of insects killed a mousey creature," Kellen said.

"Do we know anything about that mousey creature?" Narena asked.

"No," Hawthorne replied. Nyxen shook his head as he sipped his tea.

"Well," Kellen said, "we know he said Labete had sent him with a message for the king. At least that's what my father said the poor thing said just before he was murdered."

"Labete?" Narena said. "He was a Labete messenger for the king?" She shook her head. "That doesn't make any sense!"

"But it might explain why the king said he had to communicate with Labete," Hawthorne suggested.

"Wait, why doesn't it make any sense, Narena?" Kellen asked.

"Because," she said, speaking as the thoughts came to her, "insects don't act the way those did naturally. So something, or someone, must have made them do it."

"And only a Higher Spirit could have that kind of influence, right?" Hawthorne added.

"Or an Under Spirit," Nyxen put in.

"Or an Under Spirit," Narena repeated. The four looked at each other once again.

Soooonnn of Giiiniiiaaa. Saaaave uuuusss!

Nyxen jumped up. "There it is again! Did you hear that? Didn't you hear what the trees just said?"

"Whoosh?" Kellen asked, staring blankly at Nyxen.

"No! They called me son of Ginia! They know who I am! They

said, save us! It was loud and clear that time! Didn't you hear it?" he said to his sister.

"They called you by name?" Hawthorne asked.

"Yes, yes, why?"

"That's the sign," the salamander said quietly. "The trees are calling you. They really are calling you."

"The trees are calling him?" Kellen sneered. "Sure they are."

Narena stood up. "I believe him," she said, and this time she meant it. "The trees know something's wrong. They're telling us that we have to save them! We're the ones!" she said with sudden comprehension. "By the love of Yew, I understand!" She turned to her friends, her face flushed with excitement and awareness.

"We have to save the Forest. It *is* up to us!"

CHAPTER 4

"No it's not," Kellen snapped. "Our orders are to stand down. I told you that."

"Those orders don't apply to us!" Narena insisted. "Besides, if you're all standing down, who's going to enforce them?"

"I will!" Kellen exploded out of his chair. "I don't know what you're thinking you can do, but you can't! You shouldn't! I won't let you! Whatever it is, forget it!"

"Hey, back off, would you?" Nyxen exclaimed. "Haven't you noticed? We're not in school anymore, and this isn't some game of Acornball. You can't tell me or my sister what to do!"

Hawthorne put up a moist hand. "Let's all calm down," he said. "Kellen, you must realize this problem cannot be solved only by way of warriors. These massacres are beyond the jurisdiction of kings and armies. They are upsetting the whole balance of the Forest. Where can any of us go to be sure we're safe?"

"So what's your bright idea, skin-breather?" Kellen sneered.

Narena leaped up from her seat and pointed her index finger right at Kellen's nose. "Hey watch your mouth! That's my friend you're talking to, and he just lost everyone in his whole family, and his whole kingdom! Don't you have any feelings for anyone?"

Kellen stared at her blankly as she waited for a reply. Nothing. "Just as I thought," she muttered and turned away from him, sitting back down and rolling her eyes to her brother, who snickered in return.

Kellen slowly sat back down, and looked at Narena in pure disbelief, unable to hide the slight smile on the corner of his mouth. He'd known Narena all his life, but had traveled many miles from his Forest home during his training to become a warrior. So naturally, he had seen many things a normal, everyday nymph could not even fathom in their wildest dreams. But never had he come across anyone so full of hotheadedness, but beautiful in her own unique way, and yet whimsical, and yet—intelligent. Such a package was not typical in Nymph Kingdom, and Kellen had yet to come across anything to the same caliber in the rest of the Forest that he'd explored in his travels.

Most female nymphs were happy to go about their chores, doing what was expected of them to keep the kingdom flourishing, and they were really quite good at it. They rarely spoke out of turn, or even more rarely, acted in affects of the mind. And Narena did nothing but use her mind, all day, and all night. She was pure of soul, wanting only good to come of everything she encountered. And she absorbed knowledge at a rate unheard of in nymphs, granted of course, that the knowledge was of a subject that Narena was actually interested in. Kellen could not help but admire this, but still did not refrain from thinking Narena was just a bit of a pain in his hindquarters.

"Okay, okay! I hear you!" Nyxen yelled, grabbing his head. "I don't know how to do it, but we'll save you! I promise!"

Kellen looked helplessly at Nyxen, then into Hawthorne's melancholy stare. He sighed. "Well, if you're going to do... whatever it is you think you're going to do... you'll need a leader. I guess I better go along with... whatever it is you think you can do..." He glanced at Narena and straightened his shoulders. "But I'm taking point and you'd better keep up!" He stared at them, then his face changed and he tilted his head. "Now! Where are we going?"

"We're going to talk to Labete," Narena said.

"Are you joking?" Kellen said. "I don't think so. I don't think it's a good idea to leave the safety of this tree and wander around calling 'Labete! Labete!' I think that's a really good way to let the insect swarm know where we are. It's like asking to be eaten."

"We'll be watched over," Nyxen said.

The others stared at him. Narena said, "Okay, I'll ask. By who?"

"The trees. The spirits within the trees, rather."

"How do you know that?"

Nyxen rolled his eyes. "The trees told me."

Kellen said, "The trees told him. Oh, I love this plan. We're going to scurry around like a pheasant with its head cut off in search of a Higher Spirit that no one knows how to find. Great. Why haven't we already left?"

Narena had to stop herself from slapping his face. "Look, warrior boy, no one but you says you have to go with us. I believe my brother. And as for finding Labete, I know how to do that. So just back off!"

"You know how to find a Higher Spirit?"

"Yeah."

"How?"

"She read it somewhere, I'm assuming," Nyxen broke in. "I told you, she read all the books in the king's library."

"Excuse me for asking," Hawthorne chimed in, "but what did you read in all those books about finding a Higher Spirit?"

"Yeah!" Kellen said. "What's your great answer to this vast, unfathomable problem?"

Narena sighed. "It's simple. Don't you remember any of your folklore? You just have to go find the human witches!"

"Oh! Humans! Great!" Kellen sneered. "This plan just gets better and better! If the insects don't get us, and the army doesn't run us down, and Labete doesn't take his anger out on us... we can just put ourselves in the hands of the people who have tried to kill us for thousands of years. Humans! What a great plan!"

"Well it sounds about right to me!" Hawthorne declared. "And unless you have any better ideas, Kellen, I'd say this one is our best bet." He began buckling on his harness, shifting the strap to balance the heavy blade.

Nyxen headed for the kitchen. Narena went to her room to grab a knapsack that she filled with an assortment of weapons and other possible items she would need. Kellen, left alone in the foyer, muttered "Gorgon," under his breath and tightened his own quiver. The others returned quickly and Hawthorne reached for the door handle.

"One question before we leave," Nyxen said. "Where exactly are we going?"

"To the witches, remember?" Kellen replied. "We are going to the Elder Triage."

"And where is that?" Nyxen asked.

"I know," Narena piped up. "I found it in one of the books I read. They live by an oak tree on the northernmost end of the Forest, right by the outskirts of the darkest region—one of the oldest and largest in the entire Forest. Legend says that if we find the tree, it will lead us to the witches."

"All right, well, let's get a move on then," Hawthorne declared.

Kellen pulled open the door and strode forward, checking all sides for insects. Narena and Hawthorne followed closely. Nyxen paused to pull the door closed and let his fingers linger on the soft wood. "Goodbye," he whispered.

Whoosh. The tree leaves rustled, but he heard, *Not yet.*

CHAPTER 5

They were not more than three fox-tail lengths from the home when Kellen held up a fist and suddenly stopped.

"What is it?" Narena asked.

"Into the blackberry bushes!" Kellen hissed. The three companions obliged, although somewhat reluctantly so.

"What?!" Narena asked again through clenched teeth, her messy hair swooping across her concerned face.

"A guard!" Kellen pointed through the brush just above them.

"Big deal," Nyxen said.

"Last I checked, our journey wasn't royally sanctioned. If the General finds out and reports back to the king, we're done."

"Riiight. Still under Daddy's thumb," Nyxen teased.

"Wait..." Narena whispered fervently. "This could be good. I need something at the palace."

"What? No!" Kellen hissed.

"Come on, Kellen," Narena replied. "Your father's not that bad."

Kellen grunted.

"Narena, what is it you need?" Hawthorne asked softly.

"A book," Narena said. "Well, just a page from a book. But it would really help us if we had it. Especially if we're dealing with witches."

"What book?"

"*The Forest Grimoire*. The witches' home is hidden, but I know there's a spell in the *Grimoire*. I saw it once, but I need to see the page again or we'll never find them."

"All right then," Kellen grumbled. "But no mention of the book, got it?"

"Hey!" a booming voice resounded over the bush. "What are you kids doing in there? Didn't you hear the robin's song with the king's directive? Nobody is allowed at ground level! Come out this instant!"

"I know this guy. I'll handle this," Kellen hissed. "Just follow my lead."

Narena rolled her eyes.

"Did you hear me? I said *now*!"

The four slid their way out of the bramble, with Kellen practically shoving them out, and found themselves face to face with an auburn-haired palace guard with eyes so dark they were nearly black.

"Kellen!" the guard said forcefully. "What are you doing in that bush?"

"We were in the tree," Kellen said, "but..." He looked around and suddenly grabbed Nyxen by the shoulder. "But our friend fell."

Nyxen's copper eyes widened, and he awkwardly scratched a finger through his thick mane of hair.

"That's right," Hawthorne said. "He is ill. He needs a healer. We need to reach the palace. And soon, for we fear he doesn't have much time left."

Nyxen opened his mouth to protest, but Narena jabbed him in the chest with her elbow, and he coughed.

"He's been having terrible headaches lately," she said, her eyes threatening to hit him again.

Nyxen gritted his teeth. "Yeah. Headaches. Terrible. Palace." Under his breath, he growled, "I'll get you for this!"

"Our poor friend," Hawthorne said gaily, stepping up and wrapping a slimy arm around Nyxen's shoulders. "Can you help us? Please?"

"Come this way," the guard relented.

"I hate you all," Nyxen muttered, as they trudged toward the palace.

"It's okay little brother," Narena sang out, "we'll get you help!"

The group made their way past several oak tree homes, receiving some very confused glances from some housewife nymphs pinning laundry out their second story windows. When they finally reached the palace, they followed the guard down a long route corridor to the central courtyard.

The palace was built partially into a cliff side, situated delicately between the drooping roots of a centuries-old oak tree that stabilized the structure. Twinkles of light radiated through nearly every corridor and pebbles of precious gems were littered through the grayish stone that made up the palace walls. It quite the breathtaking sight and never ceased to amaze, regardless of how many times one might view it.

Narena hung back until the group had moved down the left pathway to the healer's quarters, and then quickly scurried down the opposite hall. She ducked into the library and shut the door behind her.

"Where is that book..." she whispered to herself as she scanned the shelves. "Aha! Found it!"

The book was worn with age, and covered in a thin layer of dust. Narena blew on the cover then frantically flipped through the pages. She stopped, skimmed it for a moment, then tore the sheet out in one long rip, folded it, and tucked it into her pocket. She slipped quietly out of the room and casually made her way back toward the healer's quarters.

"But Father, you don't know why I need to do this!" Kellen was saying as she entered the room.

"I can't approve of you taking off like this, son," Felide replied. "We still don't know where Rowan is, and it's definitely not safe for common folk to be out prancing around with those insects still at large!"

"You're being ridiculous!" Kellen was saying, his voice getting harder by the moment. "I'm just as good a warrior as you were at my age. I have my own command! I don't need your permission to perform my duty!"

"You may not need my permission, but you do need the king's. And remember, boy, being hot-headed enough to perform doesn't make you mature enough to keep troops alive under fire."

Father and son stood almost nose to nose. Narena had seen this dynamic before between these two, there would be no backing down from either. Without taking his eyes off his father, Kellen announced, "Come with me, Narena, Nyxen, Hawthorne. We're going to the king."

Narena, Nyxen, and Hawthorne followed Kellen down another corridor and into the dim light of a doorway. Heads held high, they confidently entered the throne room, which held an ornateness that was far less apparent in the corridors leading up to it. Amethysts, rubies, sapphires, and emeralds all danced along the walls in varying depths of color, forming a pattern that sparkled in every radiation of light. Trails of copper and silver cascaded through the gems, and right in the center of it all sat Alston upon a throne of pure gold, his chancellor Lyren at his right, and his effortlessly beautiful wife, Tiatana, seated at his left.

"And to what do I owe this pleasure today?" the king scowled, his sea-blue eyes piercing into the group as it approached him. He nodded at Felide as the General strode past the others to his son's side. "Narena. Nyxen. Kellen." He held the scowl upon Hawthorne for just a moment longer than the rest.

Felide stepped forward and bowed before his king. "Your Highness, I stumbled upon—"

"Your Majesty, I must inform you that we are leaving," Kellen announced, fully intending on interrupting his father in the manner to which he just did.

"Mm hmm. And exactly where are you going with my only daughter and my youngest son?" Alston replied, stoic as he'd ever been.

"To complete what we all know needs to be done."

"And what is that, Kellen?"

"Well—"

"My king, we simply must go! Please, Your Highness, the fate of the Forest is at stake!" Narena broke in, her desperation wholly apparent in her tone.

"My dear Narena. You think you can waltz in here, *salamander* in tow, and request my permission to do... whatever it is you think you're doing? You are sadly mistaken." Alston glared daggers into Hawthorne, and righted his posture upon his throne, clearing his throat as he shifted. "Narena, Nyxen, Kellen, and your land-crawling newt—your orders are to remain in the confines of the palace. Felide, your orders are to lock them in the library until I deem it fit to release them. If any of them tries anything, especially that slimy bug, transfer them all to the dungeon."

"But Alston—" Narena pleaded.

"Alston nothing. You will address me in the proper manner, young lady. Felide, now!"

"He's an amphibian, not a bug," Narena grumbled under her breath.

"What was that, missy?" Alston roared.

"He's an *amphibian*!" Narena shouted as Nyxen gave her a good shove in the direction of the door.

Felide motioned for the group to walk ahead of him and scooted them out of the throne room. "Father," Kellen hissed as he entered the library, "you know this is the right thing to do. For once in your life, please, disobey the king and let us go!"

"I can't do that, son," Felide said softly. "I'm sorry."

And with that, the door shut and locked, and the group was left only with silence as the sun began to set through the window.

CHAPTER 6

"Let us out!" Kellen pounded on the door.

"Just give it a rest, would you?" Nyxen sighed. "You're giving me a headache."

"Yeah, you've been doing that for hours now," Narena said from her seat in one of the armchairs across the room, facing out the window that looked upon the kingdom. "Nobody can hear us, obviously."

"It's worth a try," Kellen said through clenched teeth. "One of my guard friends could hear us. Oh, and thanks for clearing up the proper classification of a salamander. We were really all dying to know."

"I'm sorry, but if Alston wants to make me a research scientist and then ignore the knowledge I've accrued then that's his problem."

"Anyway, I doubt those guards would risk their position to deliberately disobey orders of their king," Hawthorne pointed out from the chair next to Narena's. "I think we may be on our own. And thanks, Narena." He shot her a wink.

"So what are we supposed to do then?" Nyxen asked as he paced around the room.

Hawthorne shrugged at Narena, and Kellen avoided eye contact with anyone, keeping his gaze upon the locked door.

"I wonder if that book is still here..." Narena trailed off, getting up from her chair and stretching her arms above her head. "I remember reading something when I was younger about portals you could travel through. Only problem is, you don't always have control over where you end up."

"Portals? Why would there be a portal in here?" Nyxen asked.

"She's talking about Elemeportals. I've heard of them too. A lot of the old palaces used to have them," Hawthorne said. "They send you to a location that pertains to the element button you press. But I doubt many of them work anymore. They were created by ancient magic, not the kind that governs us today. They became obsolete."

"I remember looking for one in this library when I was little," Narena continued dreamily as she wandered about the room. "When I was fourteen I tried to run away from the palace, and Alston threatened to send me through a portal to the coast if I ever tried anything like that again. So I just assumed that he had one."

"I'll take anything at this point," Kellen grunted, turning around and leaning his back upon the door, arms folded. "Whatever it takes to get us out of here."

Narena scanned the many books on the shelves, muttering the titles to herself as she moved across the room and scaled up a ladder. "Um, this may take a while," she lamented.

The library consisted of two stories, connected by a rickety ladder that swung around the perimeter of the room. Books and loose papers poured from shelves that protruded from nearly every wall, and right in the center stood a large, three-dimensional map of the entire Forest. Behind the map was a sitting area with two velvet armchairs situated around an antique desk, in front of a large window looking out on the entirety of Nymph Kingdom.

Narena closed her eyes, something she was inclined to do when faced with a problem ever since she was a young child. Closing her eyes helped her organize her thoughts and put a mental picture into Narena's head of what it was she was supposed to do. But this time, an immediate solution evaded her, almost as if her mind were surrounded by an invisible wall that would not allow any assistance within. Much like being locked in a room. Narena squeezed her eyes harder, to the point where they began to hurt.

"Anything?" Kellen asked, peering up at Narena as she stood on the ladder.

"Not yet," she replied, "but.."

"Hey, look at this!" Nyxen called out. "Something just appeared under the door!"

"What is it?" Kellen asked, helping Narena down the ladder before they made their way to where Nyxen and Hawthorne stood.

"It's a note! And... a key!"

"What does the note say?"

"It says, 'If you come back dead, I'll never forgive you.'"

"Let me see that!" Kellen snatched the note away from Nyxen, and the small, silver key clinked to the ground.

"The key!" Narena gushed. "Someone wants us to go!"

"But who?" Hawthorne asked.

"I know," Kellen replied. "This is, without a doubt, my father's handwriting. I'd recognize it anywhere." He picked up the key and tried it in the door. It opened. "Follow my lead. Stay as quiet as you possibly can.

"Now, let's get out of here!"

Chapter 7

The group safely made its way out of Nymph kingdom, using the light of the moon as a guide. After a few minutes of silently walking through the Forest, Narena caught up to Kellen.

"We want to go north," she said softly, "and we should reach the witches' tree by the early morning light. And hopefully, the only trouble we should encounter will be finding that tree at all."

"What do you mean?" Kellen inquired. "Why would we have trouble finding the tree?"

"Because it's hidden, remember?" Hawthorne piped up. "To the naked eye, anyway. I've heard there's a way to find it, and I was hoping you would know what that is, Narena."

"Um, I think I may know..." she trailed off as she fiddled in her pocket. "This page has an incantation to recite, but it doesn't say if that guarantees the tree will appear."

"So what does that mean, then?" Kellen snorted. "I thought you were more prepared than this. Sounds like you're just winging it to me."

"She'll figure it out!" Nyxen snapped. "She always does."

"So what if I am winging it?" Narena retorted. "Isn't that what you and your warrior buddies do all day? You seriously can't handle not having control, can you?"

"This is the first time I've ever had control!" Kellen snapped. "And look what little I have!"

"We'll be fine," Hawthorne cooed. "We have to trust in ourselves. If it's meant to be, it will happen. And I believe it's meant to be. We'll find it."

So the group trekked on through the rest of the night, through all the lands of the rodents and birds. They traveled over the hibernating serpents and around the foxes' dens. Past the gnome caverns and finally through the troll quarries, which were a cliff side made entirely of jagged rocks and smooth, rounded boulders in all shades of gray covered in light green moss. Twisted oak trees riddled in the same moss jammed out from the cascading rocks, shoving their way through any crevice the rocks would allow them to grow. The group did their best to remain inconspicuous as they ventured past the troll quarries, as the trolls were well-known for not enjoying a skip past their decomposing homes. It was said they guarded and harvested a magic truffle used for a truth tea, something the witches would be well-versed in, though not a matter for nymph concern.

Trolls were not as large as humans were conditioned to believe, and most were actually quite small. They appeared larger when provoked or irritated, possessing an ability to puff up their flesh and hair. Narena actually found them to be quite charming creatures, as their insight into the matters of the Forest was brilliant in her opinion. She was somewhat disappointed when none poked their spiky haired heads out to say hello to her, but could not find herself to dwell on insignificant social matters at this time.

Narena began to see flashes of light through the trees ahead of them as they walked, and as she got closer, saw that it was the clearing that marked the exact center of the Forest realm. A clearing which held one of the only opportunities to get pure, uninhibited sunlight in the Forest. It was a well-known gathering spot for treaties, and considered to be quite a sacred place. Many great ideas, both traditional and progressive, had been solidified in this clearing, the ideas evolving and shaping new Forest laws with the changing times.

"Look, there's something over there," Nyxen pointed to a black lump in the center, as the group stepped into the early morning sunlight. Kellen ducked low to the ground, quickened his pace, and rushed into the clearing before the rest. But he suddenly stopped as he reached the lump, gasped, and put his hand over his mouth.

"Hey, what gives?" Narena demanded, bumping into Kellen's back.

"It's horrible!" Kellen lamented, and the group peeked around him to witness a terrible sight.

A large, dark mass lay sprawled through the direct center, soaking up the sunlight of the day while causing the grass around it to wilt and die. Buzzing insects of all kinds soared around the mass, scoping it out but seemingly scared to land upon it. The mass itself smelled of a rotting corpse, but Narena refused to believe it to be such a thing as she ducked around Kellen and moved toward it. Only the smell prevented her from touching the mass, but she did get close enough to experience what it was, or once was, that is. A human witch. A dead human witch, for any manner of a witch would be wise to not lie upon a clearing without moving for enough time to create a massive stench. Narena felt her body cringe uncontrollably at the sight of such devastation.

She swallowed the lump that had formed in the back of her throat, and whimpered. She felt a warm hand touch gently upon the nape of her back, and her fears dissipated as she began to feel a sense of comfort unbeknownst to her previously. She could finally take in a deep breath, though one delicately filtered by her tunic over her nose due to the horrendous smell.

"What is it?" Nyxen dared ask.

"It looks like Odila if you ask me," Hawthorne replied. "She was one of the Elder Triage. Legend states she was skilled in potion concocting. Best in the land, they said!"

"Until now," Nyxen whispered.

"Who would do such a thing?" Narena whimpered.

"And what exactly did they do?" Nyxen inquired.

"It looks like she was fumed," Hawthorne said quietly. "It's when a spirit is able to manifest and manipulate enough dark energy to create a smoke ball which engulfs the victim, choking while decomposing simultaneously."

"So what does this mean? That only two witches remain for us to enlist the help of?" Kellen could not hide his frustrations any longer. "We need to come up with a concrete plan before we travel any further. Beings were killed, and who is to say we are not meddling with something so completely beyond us?"

"And what other options do we have?" Narena spoke, her orange eyes swelling with tears. "If we go back we risk this happening to our entire kingdom directly under our noses. We no longer have a choice. We must move on."

"All right. Let's keep moving, we don't want anyone to see us hanging around here anyway," Kellen replied.

"If my estimations are correct," Narena said, "we're not far from

Witch Territory. They're in the unincorporated area of the Forest, which should be coming up. I can see the darkest part of the Forest in the distance from here."

"Everyone prepare yourselves," Kellen ordered. "We're dealing with witches, so we don't know what to expect. Follow my lead."

"Follow my lead," Nyxen mocked, and looked to his sister for a response. But this time, rather than giggle at Kellen's expense with her brother, Narena simply smiled slightly, turned her face away, and kept walking. Hawthorne delayed following the group for a moment in order to perform a brief sage blessing upon the unfortunate corpse, and upon completion quickly caught up with everyone.

"Hawthorne, there you are!" Narena exclaimed. "I was just wondering where you were. Why did you stay behind?"

"Oh, just a necessary blessing to prevent Odila from rising up in our adversary's favor," the salamander replied hastily. "No need for concern."

"As long as you keep up with the rest of us, I don't care what hocus pocus you want to do in your own time," Kellen said.

"His hocus pocus may have just saved us a whole lot of grief," Narena snapped. "Since those insects were obviously possessed, who's to say that anything Labete or his minions touch could not be?"

"Clearly the witch was beyond dead. And halfway rotted into the ground, I might add. I doubt she could have done any bigger damage than spread a disease."

"I'm starting to think there's only one disease I need to be worried about," Nyxen mumbled, though loud enough for the group to hear. "And that's your attitude, warrior boy."

"My practical attitude has not only won me numerous honors, but has also saved the butts of many a warrior over the years. What has yours done, brainiac? Gotten straight marks in school?"

"Stop it this instant!" Hawthorne broke in. "I thought you were two grown male nymphs. Quit behaving like little ones, it is very unbecoming and frankly, horrible to have to listen to."

Kellen grunted and wandered ahead of the group, quickening his pace in the hopes the rest of his non-warrior comrades would be unable to keep up. But even he was taken aback when after a minute of brisk walking found him face to face with an enormous, overgrown oak tree whose branches nearly grazed the Forest floor. "Wow," he couldn't help but whisper to himself as the remaining members of the group caught up.

"Look, Kellen!" Narena said. "You found it!"

"This is the tree we're looking for?" Kellen replied.

"It has to be! It fits the description perfectly, and aside from that, it just feels right. Wouldn't you agree, Hawthorne?"

"Most certainly, my dear."

"The area where the Elder Triage's home is said to be right around here. I'll recite this incantation, and then..."

"Then what?" Nyxen asked.

"We wait for a sign."

Chapter 8

"Is something supposed to happen?" Kellen inquired in a sarcastic tone, after the group had stood awkwardly by the drooping tree for some time. "You read that incantation minutes ago! If something doesn't happen soon, I say we move on. We're wasting time, not to mention the fact that we are very easy targets right now."

"Calm down, would you?" Narena snapped. "Magic doesn't keep a sense of time or space, you know."

"Well I'd say by now, something should have happened," Nyxen chimed in. "Unless..."

Son of Ginia...

Nyxen clutched his head. "It's happening again!" he moaned. "My head!"

Son of Ginia...

"What is it?" Hawthorne asked. "A headache again?"

"My head... and the voices... they're speaking to me again..."

"What are they saying?"

"Oww..."

"Nyxen," Narena rubbed her brother's back. "We need to know what they're saying. This could be really important! Please, tell us!"

Son of Ginia. Dare you request the sight of the Elder Triage?

"That's why we're here, isn't it?" Nyxen groaned.

Only he who asks permission of the trees may his wish be granted.

"You must be joking, but okay, trees, may I please be shown the witches' lair?"

Very well. But in doing so, you must understand that you are not safe, even at the witches' home.

"Unless they're planning on boiling one of us in a stew, or something equally horrendous, I'm going to go ahead and say that's fine."

Take heed, son of Ginia.

"I will. Thanks."

The light in the Forest around the group shifted, and the drooping oak began to shimmy its form, vibrating slightly while fading into to a thick mist. It shook, then sucked into the earth with a tremendous force that nearly shook the small beings off their feet. A hole emerged and the tree was once again present, though this time in the form of a human-made house fused within the tree. A crescent moon shaped peek hole glimmered from the direct center of the sky blue dungeon-like front door, eerily welcoming the group to the home's presence.

"What are you waiting for? Knock on the door, O Brave One," Narena demanded, glaring her orange eyes into Kellen as she jokingly bowed.

"Okay, okay," Kellen replied, and stepped toward the door. He hesitated. "Right now?" He gulped.

"Working hard, earning those Forest honors, I see," Nyxen mocked.

"Come on, Kellen!" Narena hissed.

"Give me a second, would you? Even warriors have to mentally prepare themselves to face potential danger!" But before he could knock, the door violently swung open and there stood a massive, wrinkly, white-haired woman with a purple, ankle-length skirt and black and white striped socks.

"Help you?" she asked, as her good eye slid along each individual.

The witch's back was slightly hunched, and her left eye drooped, making her appear as though she was always giving a shifty eye whilst leaning closer for a whiff of one's soul. Her eyes were dark, and her hair was long, pulled behind her head in a loose, messy bun.

Kellen cleared his throat. "Hello ma'am. My name is Kellen, and these are my friends, Narena, Nyxen, and Hawthorne. We've come to you today to inquire about some goings-on in the Forest. Might we have a word?"

"You must understand I am wary of strangers."

"As are we. Please, ma'am, we could really use your help. The fate of the Forest is at stake."

"How did you find me?"

Narena stepped forward. "A book in the royal library. I've read much about your coven, ma'am. I know you can help us. You're... you're the only ones who can."

"Who speaks to the trees?"

"I... I do," Nyxen said shyly, peeking around his sister.

"How long have you been able to do that, son?" the witch asked, raising an eyebrow. "It's truly a blessed gift, you know."

"All my life I guess," Nyxen replied. "Ever since I can remember. It comes along with awful headaches, so it's more of a nuisance, if you ask me."

"'Tis to the eye of the beholder," the witch chuckled, and her energy seemed to shift. She straightened herself up and stepped backward. "All right. Come in. I knew you were coming anyway."

"How do you mean?" Kellen asked puzzlingly, as the group followed the witch into a sitting room.

"Divination, my dear," the witch replied. "Come now, have a sit." She led them into a large, human-sized sitting room.

The room was captivating, filled with deep hues of purple, cerulean, and teal that splashed vibrancy over the tapestries and velvet sitting chairs. Crystals of all sizes, shapes, and colors trickled down from the ceiling and the walls. And in the very center of it all sat a twisted, copper lamppost with intertwining, multicolored glass marbles that proudly displayed a human-head sized crystal ball.

"Wow," Narena couldn't help but whisper.

"Are they here?" a scratchy female voice called out from a back room. "Lorella?! Did they arrive?"

"Yes, yes, sister. They are here!"

"What?!"

"They're here!" Lorella screeched. "Rhoslina is a bit hard of hearing," she muttered to the group.

Rhoslina drifted into the room. She was probably only slightly younger than Lorella, but the age difference was readily apparent in her appearance, as she was dark haired with long, thick eyelashes that illuminated her periwinkle eyes. She wore extensive strands of beads and woven metal that cascaded down her bosom and over her pin-straight shoulders. Her nose was pointed with the tiniest bump on the bridge, and her mouth curled around her nose like a sleeping feline.

"I thought we agreed we were going to turn them away," Rhoslina snapped. "If Labete finds out we helped them, we'll be seeing Odila soon enough in the afterlife."

"Rhos, they have a tree whisperer. And a sage salamander. And this little lady, well, I still haven't quite put my finger on what's going on with her! They're special, my sister. They're the ones."

"Phooey!" Rhoslina replied, and sat down in one of the velvet chairs, nearly stepping on Hawthorne in the process.

"Hey, what about me?" Kellen asked. "Am I included in this compliment-fest?"

"Ah yes. You're a protector. Comes from your father. But that's not all..." The witch cleared her throat. "There's another potential here. Something from your mother's side. Something you will discover in due time."

Kellen turned bright red. "All right," he grunted. "Didn't know I was getting a psychic reading."

Lorella looked him dead in the eye. "I don't know if you're ready for a real reading from me, mister. Wouldn't want to embarrass you in front of the one you desire."

"Huh? I don't know what you're talking about!" Kellen argued.

"And it better not be me," Nyxen grunted under his breath and looked at Narena, who was still gazing around the room with wide eyes. Whether or not she had been listening was questionable.

"Okay, that's enough, Lorella. Let's just give them what they need so they can be on their way," Rhoslina broke in.

"Now what kind of hostess would I be if I didn't offer them some food and drink? And it's getting late, I'm wondering if they should rest up here for awhile before we send them off."

Rhoslina threw up her arms. "Do what you want. Just come fetch me when we're ready for the divination." And with that, she left the room.

Lorella motioned for the group to follow her into the kitchen, where she provided them with a feast of human proportions. Steamed kale, potatoes, carrots, and beets. Sweet rolls, rice, and broccoli. A nymph's favorite medley of diet, and all said an incantation of blessing before jumping in to the food. Even Hawthorne was given a saucer of worms and larvae, which he devoured before anyone else was halfway complete. Though the feast was plentiful and all were thoroughly satisfied, few words were spoken at dinner.

After all bellies were full, Lorella scooted them back to the sitting room where she placed them in a circle around the lamppost, seating herself in a purple velvet armchair directly in front of the crystal ball. After three attempts at calling in Rhoslina, the witch finally arrived and sat across from her sister.

"Okay, are we all ready?" Lorella said. "Clear your minds of all clutter, and focus solely on the issue at hand, and the questions you want answered. Now close your eyes, we will begin the divination."

CHAPTER 9

"Why do we need to perform a divination?" Kellen asked, annoyed. "Why can't you just tell us what we need to know so we can be on our way?"

Lorella chuckled. "Silly nymph. Do you even know who your enemy is?"

"A swarm of insects."

"If only it were that easy. Wipe out a swarm of insects and save the Forest, right? Unfortunately the situation is far more dire than what you'd expect."

"Who is it, then?!"

Lorella crouched down to Kellen's level, and glared right through him, twitching her bad eye. "Your enemy was once your protector," she said in a deep, gruff voice. "It is Labete."

"I knew that," Kellen huffed. "We just weren't sure, is all."

"But why?!" Narena squeaked. "Why would Labete suddenly turn bad? Why would he do this to the Forest that he looked after for so long?"

"There was a great disruption in the balance of good and evil," Lorella replied. "Labete was negatively influenced by Agrimon, so turned to the other side. This falling of the Forest has been a long time coming. Even before your useless king was appointed. I'm sure Gorgon had been waiting centuries to enact something like this."

"So what are we supposed to do, then?"

"That's what we're trying to find out with this divination. We need to know where Labete is hiding out. The longer he stays negative, the more species he will either influence or destroy. And I'm not even sure if he can be brought back to the positive after this."

"So let's find out where he is, then," Kellen said.

"This isn't some warrior jog through the outskirts of Nymph Kingdom, you know," Lorella snapped. "We're talking about the destruction of a Higher Spirit here. Something like this has never, ever been attempted in the entire history of the Forest's existence!"

"And who is to know if you will even succeed!" Rhoslina chimed in. "Labete could likely destroy all of you simply by thinking it so!"

"We can't let that happen," Hawthorne piped up. "Labete must be stopped, even if I perish in the process. I owe it to my species."

"Let's begin then, shall we?" Lorella said. She waved her hands over the crystal ball, and began to speak an incantation aloud. As she continued to call out, her voice started to sound less and less like her own, and her words became more and more incomprehensible. Then her body shook around violently as the crystal began to show a swirling white and gold cloud. Little by little, the cloud articulated into the image of a vast, triumphant mountain, a familiar sight for the members of the group.

"It's the mountain," Rhoslina whispered. "I should have known. Labete is at the peak of Lapis Mountain."

"So... I guess we're climbing a mountain, then," Nyxen groaned.

Lorella's voice stopped and her body slumped in her chair. Rhoslina rushed over to her and poured some water into her mouth. "Oh my, that was quite a trance, wasn't it?" Lorella muttered, slowly righting herself. "Now, what did the crystal show?"

"Lapis Mountain," Rhoslina replied. "Labete is hiding out near the top. He... he must be guarding... you know... to make sure he doesn't wake up."

"Who?" Kellen broke in. "Who's asleep?"

"The Yew," Lorella replied. "That's another reason the Forest is out of balance. The Yew is asleep. Been that way for years now. And the funny thing is, the only way I know of for you to destroy Labete would involve you waking the Yew and prompting him to help you."

"Because only a Higher Spirit can destroy another Higher Spirit, right?" Narena asked.

"That's right."

"So you didn't know the Yew was asleep?" Rhoslina addressed the nymphs. "Gosh, those faeries really weren't kidding when they said nymphs were oblivious creatures."

"It's not their fault," Hawthorne said. "I for one am not surprised at all to learn they didn't know about the Yew. Consider who their king is."

"Hey, if King Alston thought it was necessary for us to know something important, I'm sure he would share that information," Narena chimed in. "He probably just didn't want to worry us."

"Or protect you, obviously," Rhoslina mumbled.

"So let me get this straight," Kellen broke in. "The Yew is asleep on the top of Lapis Mountain. Labete is also there, guarding the Yew from awakening. But in order to destroy Labete, we would need to wake the Yew.

Piece of cake." He rolled his eyes.

"Simple enough, indeed!" Lorella declared, getting up from her seat and walking toward a long hallway. "And let's not forget about the sacrifice, of course. One will need to be made in order to complete the spell to awaken the Yew. But you have plenty of time to worry about that," she said quickly. "All right, now that the divination is complete, allow me to prepare a room for you four to sleep in until morning light."

"We must be going now," Kellen said curtly. "We have no time to waste."

"I'm afraid you do," Lorella replied, opening the front door to a thundering rainstorm outside. "Don't worry, it will all be clear tomorrow morning. Come now, let me show you where you'll be sleeping."

CHAPTER 10

"Here we are!" Lorella said in a sing-song voice. She opened the door to a beautifully yellow accented room, with small clear crystals hanging from the ceiling that reflected shadowy, iridescent rainbows from the candlelight upon the pale sunflower-colored walls. A single bed with hand-carved, wooden posts was centered against a wall aside a small, stained-glass window.

Lorella walked over to the bed and fiddled around with the covers with her back turned. When she turned to face the four, she stepped aside to reveal four tiny nymph-sized beds with fine draperies engulfing the sleeping quarters.

"The purple one is yours, Narena." the witch said quietly as Narena beamed and approached her specially-made bed.

"Thank you Lorella! It's beautiful."

"You are very welcome. Now, Hawthorne, you will find I made your bed out of a clean dish filled with shallow water and dirt so your amphibious body can remain moist. Kellen and Nyxen, you two are over here at the foot of the bed."

"Thank you, Lorella," the three boys replied in unison.

"Now make yourselves comfortable, and try to get some sleep. You'll need it tomorrow."

And with that, Lorella drifted out of the room, her long wispy skirt nearly trapping itself in the door as she swung it open only enough for her witch body to sweep through the doorway and disappear.

"I wonder what she meant by 'a sacrifice needs to be made'," Nyxen whispered as the four crawled into their specially-made beds and a bolt of lightning lit up the room.

"Probably exactly what it sounds like," Narena replied. "I'm just hoping it doesn't mean a life needs to be sacrificed. I know I will have an issue with it, if it is."

"It probably is," Hawthorne said. "What other sacrifices are there?"

"No one is being sacrificed," Kellen grunted. "We'll worry about that when it arises. For now, let's try to rest up so we can think clearly tomorrow."

Narena laid down, pulled her blanket up over her ears as the thunder roared outside, and closed her eyes. After drifting off to sleep for a short while, she suddenly jolted awake to the sound of scratching around her bed quarters. She opened her eyes to find a moving shadow outside of the curtain, and while she yearned to call out to the shadow, found herself unable to speak. The shadow grew closer, became larger in her line of vision, and Narena now found herself unable to breathe. Just as she realized she was going to need to scream to wake the witches, a pair of glistening green eyes peeked into the curtain and looked upon her.

"Kellen!" Narena hissed, as she was now able to speak. "What are you doing over here?"

"I was worried about you," he replied. "I heard you speaking frightfully in your sleep, and you were thrashing around."

"Oh, I must not have noticed," Narena said awkwardly, and immediately realized this was very out of the ordinary for her. To not have a quick-witted response!

"Of course you didn't," Kellen whispered, a grin spanning across his handsome face. "You were asleep, silly."

"Beings have bad dreams, you know," Narena said, squinting her eyes. "They're not going to kill me."

"You've definitely got your father's warrior gene in you, that's for sure."

"What is that supposed to mean?"

"Your combative nature. You have the fight within you. You should have been a warrior."

"I prefer matters of the mind, thank you very much."

"It's a shame. I bet you could have almost been as good a warrior as me."

Narena grinned. "Well that's not difficult to do."

"I'm serious!"

"I know, I'm just kidding around with you. I'm sure you're used to it, you know, girls getting awkward around you and what not."

"I'm not sure what you mean."

"Never mind."

"I don't care about them." Kellen tilted his head to make eye contact with Narena, despite the fact that she was doing her best to shield her glance away from him. "I only like one girl."

"You a flutterbum?" Narena joked, using a term that nymphs used to describe one who had an affinity for fancying faeries.

"One nymph. One girl nymph."

"Hmm, who could it possibly be?"

Narena looked into Kellen's eyes, and both allowed smiles to overtake their faces. Then they both quickly averted their eyes downward, caught themselves, and laughed. She crawled closer to him, and soon found herself engulfed in his never-ending arms. He held her and caressed her arms for a moment, but just as Narena turned to kiss him, the two were startled by loud crash, then a boom as a tree branch burst through the window and slid all the way into the room, just narrowly missing exploding into the bed.

Narena screamed, and Kellen leaped up and ran back to his bed, grabbing his bow and arrows before returning to shield her from whatever was entering their space. The witches stormed into the room, and Hawthorne scurried out of his dish. Nyxen slowly emerged from his bed, and gave his sister a disgusted look as he noticed her lying with Kellen.

The witches rushed into the room and dashed to the bed to see if everyone was all right. Kellen bumbled through an explanation as to why he and Narena were still awake, but Narena's eyes were fixated on a small, nymph-sized figure standing in the very corner of the room, somewhat sheathed by the fallen tree. She then found that once again, she could not move, scream, and could just barely breathe.

"Narena? Narena my dear, what is it?" Rhoslina gently shook the female nymph by the shoulders upon noticing her stare.

Narena was able to gulp, but kept her eyes upon the figure. Rhoslina's eyes followed Narena's, and her soft, caring demeanor instantly changed to one of a defensive panic.

"Tell us what you want, Spirit!" the witch demanded. "Or be gone your wretched existence from my sight!"

The shadow began to manifest itself more articulately, and as it came into view, started to show the likeness of a handsome nymph warrior, with shimmering, golden blonde hair and sharp, blue eyes that stared directly into Kellen's.

"Rowan," Kellen whispered.

Rowan nodded slightly to his former comrade, but his face suddenly twisted in horror as a swirling began at his feet, traveling up his spirit body, transforming him from his nymph likeness to that of a twisted creature; his teeth enlarged into fangs hanging like icicles from his black, foaming lips, and his back hunched, angling over his now oversized curling feet. Coarse hair of pure darkness spiked out of every inch of his being, and he heaved in a way that no spirit should.

Kellen began to approach the creature, slowly taking silent steps across the room and climbing upon a fallen branch.

"Rowan," Kellen said, "what has happened to you, my friend?"

"I am now what I was destined to become," Rowan's voice was deep and growling. "I became what he wanted me to be. I have reached what the Forest needs me to be!"

"A monstrous beast?! Rowan, you are a *nymph*! A warrior nymph! The only son of the king!"

"I am no longer one of you. I embraced the dark entities on that fateful day. You escaped with your life. I am enslaved to mine for all eternity."

"But you must allow us to release your spirit! You are no longer living!" Rhoslina cried out.

"I was not living before. Now I shall live forever!" Rowan burst through the tree, slamming through Kellen's body and knocking him to the ground before fleeing out the window.

Narena ran to Kellen. He was all right, though looked as though the wind had been knocked out of him. She helped him up, and the two stood, staring at the window, still clutching tightly to one another.

"He knows your intentions now," Lorella said. "He took a little bit of Kellen's energy with him when he passed through him."

"Indeed," Rhoslina chimed in. "Your quest now consists of much more dire circumstances. I'm afraid that now you carry targets on your backs. I think it's best you all begin to prepare to leave, it's time for you to be on your way."

"But wait, how are we supposed to awaken the Yew?" Narena asked helplessly, as the witches began shoving the group into the hallway.

"You have a tree whisperer with you," Lorella replied, scooting Narena toward where Rhoslina had opened the front door and was standing there, scowling. "Trust that your direction will be given to you from the trees. Listen to him. He's very important."

"Yeah!" Nyxen cheered as he was shoved onto the witches' front stoop. "Listen to me for once, will you?"

"But when are the trees going to..." Narena trailed off in her final push to the outside, whipping her body around to see the door slam shut behind her. Then the witches' home disappeared completely.

CHAPTER 11

"Thank the Yew, at least it stopped raining," Nyxen said as the group began to walk away.

"Yeah, that's kind of odd, isn't it?" Narena said. "That it would just happen to stop after Rowan leaves."

"Seems about right," Kellen muttered. "I've always known Rowan to be very dramatic in life. Guess he's even more over-the-top in death. If we weren't so worried about Labete I'd say Rowan would be one to watch out for."

"Everything is getting more intense," Narena said quietly. "I can feel it."

"That it is," agreed Hawthorne. "Let's take heed as we travel. Something definitely feels off to me as well."

The group walked for quite awhile in silence, but the distant sound of slurping liquid began to resonate in the trees, amidst the almost silent whistle of the wind dancing through branches and leaves. As they continued further, the harmonics blended together to create an opus of melody orchestrated by the sound of the earth's desperate plea for acknowledgment.

Son of Ginia.

Nyxen fell to his knees. "Ow, it's happening again." The rest of the group stopped.

Follow the creek, son of Ginia.

"They say to follow the creek."

"Here it is," Hawthorne pointed down a short, rocky incline. "Upstream, yes? Are you able to ask the trees for confirmation?"

The sage speaks the truth.

"They say you're right, Hawthorne."

"Follow me," Kellen said, and began leading the group down the incline. He offered his coarse, thick hand to Narena, but she shook her head at him and held back, sliding on the sides of her boots down on her own. Kellen playfully rolled his eyes at her, while cracking his signature slight smile.

Narena bounced her way down to the bank and splashed some water on her face. "Good thing we don't have to worry about kalpies in this creek anymore," she lamented, then looked up to see Kellen's horrified expression. "Oh! Gorgon! I'm sorry, Kellen."

"It's fine," Kellen muttered, and quickened his pace, wandering down the bank of the creek and out of earshot.

"Explain to me again what kalpies were, Hawthorne," Nyxen asked once Kellen had disappeared from view. "I only know what Narena used to tell me as a child to scare me into doing her chores for her."

"Not what they were," Hawthorne said between sips of creek water. "What they are. They still exist, but only in the unincorporated areas of the Forests. The ones not under kingdom rule. They're forbidden from kingdoms."

"Why?"

"They're a menace. They pop out of bodies of water and try to lure you near the water's edge. If they succeed, they drown you. Beings molded by Gorgon himself, no doubt."

"How do you defeat one?"

"Trickery," Narena broke in. "You make them tilt their head, which is hollow and filled with a pool of water. If you make them dump their water out, they have to go back in the creek. Then you can run away."

"They sound creepy," Nyxen said.

"They're not just creepy. They're extremely dangerous," Hawthorne replied. "Let's keep moving and catch up to Kellen. We don't want to get separated."

But Kellen had scurried quite a ways ahead of the group, and found that he could no longer hear their muffled conversation, so decided to sit on a patch of moss by the bank and wait for them to catch up. He closed his eyes for a brief moment, and was starting to drift into a nap when he was disturbed by a harrowing sound behind him.

A dank, heaving breath echoed in his ear as goosebumps began to riddle his tanned skin. Kellen turned slowly, hand upon his blade, to find himself face to face with a kalpie, its black beady eyes glaring back at him, surrounded by a slippery, triangular head that was hollowed out at the top. The creature's stomach protruded out, and its limbs were long and gangly.

"You'd better back away from me," he growled at the creature. "You have no idea how long I've wanted to destroy one of you."

"But how will you destroy me while you're digesting in my stomach?" the kalpie hissed.

Kellen swung his body around and swiped his blade in the kalpie's direction, slicing its cheek but not stopping its advance. The kalpie lurched forward quickly, latching its teeth into the shoulder of his tunic but luckily missed tearing into his flesh.

Kellen tried to shake the creature off of him, which only caused the kalpie to grab at his free arm. He heard Narena's voice scream out for the others to come help, but just as the sound of his comrades' pounding footsteps grew closer Kellen was able to swing his arm around to stab the kalpie in its side.

The creature wailed and bent over, clutching its wound and dumping the water in the hollow of its head onto the ground. Kellen took the opportunity to slice the creature once again, this time across its stomach, spilling its entrails onto the Forest floor at his feet. The kalpie slumped to the Forest floor, its eyes glazed over, and laid motionless. Kellen sighed.

"Wow, Kellen," Narena whispered, having crept to his side after the kalpie's fall. "You are quite the warrior indeed!"

"Yeah, I wouldn't want to mess with you," Nyxen chimed in.

"That kalpie didn't belong here," Hawthorne spoke up, a panic in his voice. "There could be more, we best move on. And quickly. Away from the creek if we can."

So the group continued on, venturing away from the bank of the creek, and this time much more cautious and aware of their surroundings than they were prior to the kalpie encounter. Since they had left the Elder Triage's home in the dark, early morning hours, the sun began to peek through the morning fog right about when they stumbled onto a "faery trail", a pathway commonly traveled by their winged kin, that spanned through the creek and up the sides of the bank, heading upstream.

"Faeries often go to the base of the mountain," Hawthorne explained. "They pick up precious gems and stones from the mining trolls for trade with other species."

"Then this is a good route to follow," Kellen replied, placing his hand upon the small of Narena's back as they stepped.

As they continued walking, Narena noticed a beautiful gathering of honeysuckle, a flower bush she adored and had always harbored a special connection with as her, and her mother's favorite smell. She harbored many a memory of gathering bushels of honeysuckle with her mother, and the scent alone brought her back to a time that she so desperately wished to return to, but never again could.

She briefly stopped to pick a few of the beautiful yellow flowers, and as she bent over she felt a brisk wind breeze pass her through her hair rapidly, followed by Kellen tackling her onto the ground, screaming for them to duck and cover. Just as they did, another breeze rampaged past Nyxen's head, just grazing his pointed ear and drawing a drop of blood.

"Arrows!" Kellen screamed, and turned to the direction the arrows were coming from, pulling an arrow out of his pack and moving toward the tree in which the arrows seemed to come from. "Stop! We are friends of the Forest! I order you in the name of King Alston to desist or I shall return fire!" He held the arrow in his bow at the ready and circled his body around at the surrounding trees.

"Alston?!" a small squeaky female voice replied from above. "Why would I stop in the name of Alston?" A female warrior faery with chestnut brown hair, a tiny, pointed nose, and sparkling periwinkle eyes descended from a tree with a smirk. "Nobody respects him anymore. In fact, why would you even still be loyal to such a Forest traitor? Don't you know he's been in cahoots with Labete since the beginning of this falling?" The faery giggled. "You nymphs are in way over your heads. Destined to walk on the dirt and accomplish nothing but aid in the falling of your own Forest by way of your king. Ha!"

"How dare you soil the name of nymphs. Whatever King Alston does in no way represents us if what you speak is true, Faery. We are on a quest to save the Forest," Nyxen said forcefully. "You faeries all think that you can fly around the Forest, running your mouths, and shooting arrows at innocent travelers. I hope you intend on using some of your white magic to heal my bleeding ear from your arrow."

The faery smirked, and floated down in front of Nyxen, standing with her pointed nose grazing onto his. "What is your name, nymph?" she demanded.

"I am Nyxen. And this is my sister Narena," Nyxen replied, his voice now shaky. The faery's eyes moved to Narena, and her demeanor suddenly matched her soft appearance. After a brief pause, Nyxen continued. "And this is Kellen, a warrior nymph, and Hawthorne, a salamander friend."

"Your sister, huh?" the faery lamented, gazing off into space. "I had a brother once. Gosh, what I wouldn't give to have him back."

"What happened to him?" Narena asked softly, stepping closer to the faery.

"I'm not entirely sure. He went off on a quest, and never returned. That was a long time ago, he was one of the very first to try to investigate and stop this falling. We faeries were summoned first—since of course... you know... because of... the obvious advantages to being a faery..." she trailed off, as if distracted, and stared off into the sky for a brief moment. But as quickly as she drifted away, the faery's attention shot back to reality. "I just wish I could know what happened to him, my intuition tells me he might be alive but I just don't know anymore! The magic of the Forest has waned since this terrible time began, and I find myself to have less and less accuracy with it."

"So what are you doing here, by yourself, then?" Nyxen could not take his eyes off the faery.

"Well, Nyxen, I guess you could say that I am lost, though not that that this is any of your concern nor business." The faery stuck out her tongue at Nyxen, which was so unexpected that he couldn't help but laugh.

"How on earth did you manage to get yourself lost?" Nyxen asked.

"I was supposed to be going to your kingdom, actually. A few of us were sent by our king to talk some sense into yours. I stopped to smell these honeysuckle bushes for awhile, take the *tiniest* nap, then I wake up and *bam!* Everyone's gone. I decided to wait here and catch them on the way back, since I doubt it will take much before Alston casts them out of his kingdom, like he's done to so many others before us." The faery rolled her periwinkle eyes, which were accented by long, thick, black eyelashes.

"Unfortunately for you, I doubt they will be back," Kellen broke in. "The Forest is pretty dangerous now. No one is safe."

The faery looked at Kellen in shock for a second, then burst into tears.

"Now look what you've done," Nyxen snapped. "You like making girls cry, army boy?" He walked over to the faery and put his arm around her, patting her shoulder. "I'm sure your brother is fine, um, faery."

"It's Sebillon," the faery replied, turning her head quickly to bury her teary face into a very surprised looking Nyxen. "I'm a warrior... one of the only girl warriors in my kingdom."

"Don't worry, Sebillon," Nyxen said. "Everything will be all right."

"Don't lie to her," Kellen snapped. "We don't know that."

"Don't be so mean," Narena said, and Kellen furrowed his brow, but said nothing in reply. "Why don't you come along with us, Sebillon?"

"What?!" Kellen hissed. "Are you crazy? Did you forget that she just tried to kill us, literally, two seconds ago?"

"She should come with us," Hawthorne finally spoke. "I feel it."

"You have got to be kidding me," Kellen groaned. "What's the point of me even having rank if no one listens to me anyway? Fine, do what you want. I'm moving on now, so you can all either follow me or stay here and rot." He started to walk away, but turned slightly to nod at Narena.

"What do you say? Want to come with us?" Nyxen asked.

"Sure. Where are you going?"

"To Lapis Mountain. We're going to awaken the Yew and stop Labete once and for all!"

"Wow, that's the most excitement I've seen out of you since we started our quest," Narena teased.

Nyxen blushed. "Well, you coming Sebillon?"

"I wouldn't be much of a warrior if I said no, now would I?" the faery replied with a smile. "Let's go, it looks like Kellen is already well on his way."

Narena, Nyxen, and Hawthorne began following Kellen once more down the faery trail, with Sebillon fluttering above closely behind. And with that, the four became five.

CHAPTER 12

"So, Sebillon, explain to me again what you know about Alston's part in this falling," Nyxen questioned the faery as they walked, his face red as a holly berry.

"I only know what I've been told," Sebillon replied. "Mostly that Alston is a traitor to the Forest, has no right to be king, and the only reason he *is* king is because of a conspiracy among the Higher and Under Spirits. Labete chose him to cause this chaos in the Forest, and now he won't do anything to help anyone."

"Sounds about right," Nyxen grunted under his breath.

"We faeries think that Labete has to be possessed," Sebillon continued. "Either by Agrimon or Gorgon himself. The underworld must be seething in anger..."

"Gosh, it sure would have been nice if the faeries had relayed this information to the Nymph Army," Kellen broke in, the sarcasm readily apparent in his tone. "Maybe we could have talked some sense into Alston."

"I doubt it would have done any good," Hawthorne chimed in. "Alston is merely a pawn in a bigger game, one that I don't think we, as beings of the earth, can understand. Not in life, anyway."

"Everybody knows about this," Sebillon replied haughtily. "It's not like it's some big Forest secret. Ever since Alston was crowned, the other kingdoms basically washed their hands of him."

"Oh, is that why faeries treat nymphs so terribly? I thought that was just an unwarranted superiority complex," Kellen said.

"My kind are the only species that don't mask our true feelings. We wear our hearts on our sleeves. We're not fake."

"Could have fooled me," Kellen snapped.

"Knock it off, would you? She's helping us, isn't she?" Nyxen said as he trudged behind the others. "Your incessant arguing is giving me a headache."

"A headache-headache?" Narena asked hopefully. "Or a tree-whispering headache?"

"Oww..." Nyxen clutched his skull.

Son of Ginia...

"Here it comes again..."

"What's happening to him?" Sebillon asked.

"He's tree-whispering," Narena replied.

"Oh?" Sebillon looked confused, but did not question any further.

Son of Ginia. You must now seek the Gray Witch of the Willow....

"Who's the Gray Witch of the Willow?" Nyxen asked.

"I know!" Narena cried out. "That's Nessaba! I read about her numerous times!"

"Well that's who we need to find before we go to the mountain, apparently she's pretty important to our quest," Nyxen replied, his headache starting to fade. "She's in a willow tree somewhere."

"Not just anywhere!" Narena said. "Willows aren't native to this Forest. Nessaba is such a powerful witch that she transported her entire tree home from the swamp where she used to live. Far, far away from here. Years worth of travel away."

"So she's not a native witch to this Forest, then?" Kellen asked. "Wait, is she the one that's mentioned in the study portion of warrior training?"

"That's very possible. She's famous, err, notorious, rather."

"For what?"

"Gosh, you really didn't pay attention in studies, did you? She's fluent in black magic. Knows white magic too. The darker aspect of what she knows seals her notoriety."

"What kind of dark things has she done?" Nyxen asked.

"Let's just say she's dealt with her fair share of entities. And she's apparently hundreds of years old, but doesn't look it at all."

"Wait, isn't she the witch who wiped out the ogres that used to live in this Forest?" Kellen piped up. "She's a murderer, Narena!"

"So are you, if you want to look at things from a literal standpoint," Narena snapped.

"Why would she wipe out the ogres?" Nyxen asked.

"Good question. That I don't know," Narena replied. "But if the trees said to find her, we're finding her. Period."

"Shh!" Kellen hissed suddenly, and ducked low to the ground. "I think I hear something big coming our way. Everybody stand down!"

"Hide in here!" Hawthorne cried, ducking behind a thick piece of redwood bark that was propped up against an egg-shaped rock. The other four hastily followed.

The group peeked out onto the faery trail only to witness a sight of pure panic. A stampede of animals, eyes wide in fear and desperation, stormed past the beings' shelter, tearing up brush and ripping up the earth as their hooves and claws scraped into the ground to push their bodies further from whatever imminent danger they were fleeing from. Wings flapped as the birds they were attached to shrieked in terror. Deer, foxes, rabbits, skunks, raccoons, lizards, snakes, and even turtles ran fervently to the best of each one's abilities. Behind them, the group could only witness flashes of black shadows, looking to be in the likenesses of the animals fleeing, persistently drifting at a steady pace behind the stampede.

The five beings stared in shock, and tried to remain silent as the animals rampaged by. When it had finally passed completely, they turned to one another.

"What on earth was that?" Sebillon whispered.

"Did you see those dark shadows?" Nyxen shuddered.

"The Forest is getting worse," Hawthorne said. "Those shadows are the evilness within every soul. Labete must be pulling that part out, destroying the balance within each being. He's well on his way to negatively influencing every species. We don't have much time."

"No, indeed you don't!" a scratchy, yet squeaky female voice resounded from the back of the shelter.

The five whipped around to the darkness of the crevice between the rock and bark behind them, and found themselves looking upon a blackened silhouette crouching in the corner. The figure crept forward into the small rectangle of light passing into the shelter, and the five looked upon a small (though roughly about the size of nymph), pointy eared, reddish-brown bat.

"Identify yourself, bat!" Kellen had unsheathed the blade from his thigh and had it pointed directly between the black, chiropteran eyes that peered back at him.

The bat leaned forward menacingly, chuckled gaily, and opened its mouth, baring two elongated, razor-sharp fangs that dripped saliva. "Why, I am Nessaba of course."

Chapter 13

Kellen shoved Narena behind him and readied his hand on his blade. "Get behind me," he hissed to the others, to which Nessaba laughed.

"Silly nymphs," she cackled. "Anyone unknown is an enemy. Just like your king." She crawled her way around the group and out into the open Forest. She then stood upright, waved her arm in a circular motion around her body, and promptly transformed into her normal self, which happened to be a very lovely middle-aged-looking woman with shoulder-length, auburn brown hair and a long, square-shaped nose.

She was tall and lean, though had terrible posture, and her movements continued to mirror that of a bat despite her human morph. Her eyes were orange to the likeness of Narena's, though no other aspect of her appearance matched any other similarity.

"Come now, come come!" Nessaba sang. "Out of there, quickly now!"

The group wearily exited their hiding place and stood under the witch, looking up, except for Sebillon, who fluttered at her knee level.

"Now," the witch spoke again, "tell me your names." Kellen hesitated, and the rest of the group followed his lead. "You must know I was foretold of your desire to find me."

"Yes, we were trying to find you," Narena stammered from behind Kellen. "The... the trees told us to."

"How marvelous!" Nessaba said. "Which one of you speaks to them?"

"I do," Nyxen spoke up.

"And who is 'I'?"

"Nyxen."

"And your friends?"

"Well, um, this is Kellen..."

"Yes, yes the feverish one."

"...and here's Sebillon..."

"The faery, yes."

"and the salamander is Hawthorne..."

"Yes, yes, salamander."

"and over here is my sister, Narena."

"The spunky one! Great! How grand! Okay, now that we've gotten acquainted, follow me this way!" Nessaba began to wander off toward a thicker patch of trees off in the horizon. The group looked around at each other, and Narena shrugged.

"We wanted to find her, didn't we?" she asked. "Might as well follow."

"What if she wants to eat us?" Kellen hissed. "We already know she has no problem killing out an entire species of ogres, what makes you think she wouldn't do the same to us?"

"Ahh, tis such a blessing to have the hearing of a bat," Nessaba called back. "Think what you want about me, but if you must know I have no intention of eating you. Or killing you at all, for that matter. But decide what you will! Just know that by the time you've decided, there might no longer be a Forest to save!" She began to prance off again, but this time, the group followed.

"Where are we going?" Narena asked softly, catching up to the witch's ankles.

"To my house," Nessaba replied. "I need some things there. Don't worry, we're not too far. My stove should be nice and heated by now. I put plenty of wood in before I left."

"What?!" Nyxen cried.

"Ha ha, just joking around with you. You little beings are so easy to play with, you see."

"Get whatever you need while we wait outside!" Kellen ordered, to which Nessaba turned her head to show her overly amused expression.

"I told you I'm not going to eat you," she frankly replied. "But if you wish to wait outside rather than enjoy the warmth and safety of my magically protected home, so be it."

"I don't know about you guys, but I'm certainly going in!" Sebillon piped up.

"You little ones wouldn't provide me much of a meal anyway. Too much bones, not enough meat. Ha ha!"

"Yeah, you can wait outside and keep watch, warrior boy," Nyxen sneered.

"Just come in with us," Narena whispered to Kellen. "I don't want you out by yourself anyway. Please?"

"Hrmph. Only 'cause you asked."

"Here we are!" Nessaba sang, and waved her arms around, muttering some incomprehensible words. "Now, my dears, cover your eyes!"

A low hum of a vibration slightly shook the ground under the beings' feet, and in a sudden flash of light, a large, drooping willow tree appeared in front of the group. The tree was old, as was apparent in its appearance, and its limbs hung so low they could almost tickle the earth under one's toes, much like the Elder Triage's oak tree.

"Home, sweet home!" Nessaba declared, opening the door and scooting everyone inside. "Don't be shy, make yourselves comfortable." She scurried into the kitchen and began making noise.

Nessaba's home was humble by any means, and definitely looked as though it were thoroughly lived in, and had been so for a very long time. Books, papers, fabrics, and various other clutter was littered throughout the front rooms, the chairs and shelves pouring waterfalls of disarray that loomed over the small beings like an impending avalanche. Narena looked around at the helpless mess, and wondered where she planned on resting her behind in such disorder. Her friends appeared to be pondering that very sentiment, so the group simply stood in awe from the foyer.

Nessaba returned to the front room with a tray of food and tea and placed it on a table, atop a mountain of crumpled papers. She brushed some debris off a burgundy armchair, walked to the group and picked them all up at once, pushing their bodies close to her bosom.

"Put us down!" Kellen wailed, clenching his fists. "We can walk on our own!"

"But it's so much easier this way!" Narena squealed, looking down at how far the ground was from where her legs dangled freely.

"Ah, I wanted to save you some time," Nessaba laughed as she let the beings drop onto the chair. Kellen leaped back toward her nose and took a swing at it.

"Listen, you witch! I'm not dealing with your nonsense for one more second until you clear something up!"

"What is that, my dear?" the witch replied with a smile.

"What did you do to those ogres? Did you murder them all? Why did you do that?!"

Nessaba chuckled. "Trust me, the Forest is better off."

"What is that supposed to mean? Or is that just you justifying killing other living beings for no reason?"

"It means, if not for those ogres being wiped out, the Forest would be worse off now than it is currently."

"Elaborate, or we're gone."

"Isn't it you who needs my help?"

"I'm this close to walking."

"Witches are a very important part of keeping the Forest's balance. That's why we tend to only specify in certain traits. I, for example, excel in the art of exorcisms, or things of spiritual matter. Lorella, who you may have heard of, is skilled in the art of divination. Her sister, Rhoslina, is spells..."

"And?!"

"Kellen, stop!" Narena cried. "Let her finish!"

"And... my dears, the ogres were possessed by dark entities sent by Gorgon himself. With instructions to destroy the beings of light in this Forest."

"So what? We could have fought them off!" Kellen declared.

"At the time this happened, there weren't armies like there are today. It was a simpler time, a more innocent time. If those ogres hadn't been stopped... well... none of you would be alive today. Your ancestors never would have survived to create you."

"This had to have been way long ago," Hawthorne chimed in. "Little is known about this event even in sage history. You must have seen it all!"

"Indeed, things I do not care to relive, mind you. Not many survived that ordeal. But this Forest has long forgotten it, and has come back from the near brink of extinction. I intend to not allow things to reach that point again!"

"How have you survived this long, Nessaba?" Narena asked.

"Longevity spell, of course. All witches have them performed during their apprenticeships. We can only die if we are killed," the witch replied. "We've already lost a valuable member of our coven, and I certainly don't intend to lose any more."

"See?" Narena whispered to Kellen. "She *is* good. Now will you take a breath and rest for a moment? You're much cuter when you're calm."

"You're cuter when you're quiet," Kellen muttered.

Narena looked deeply at Kellen to gauge a visible response. None. She began to think that maybe he was a nymph warrior descended from the stone lineage. He gave no discernible reaction to very much at all, unless he was upset by a situation that seemed out of his control. But there was a part of him, given away by the slightest twinkle of his eye, that caused Narena to think he thought of her as someone different. Someone special. And as she recalled moments throughout her childhood where Kellen would always seem to randomly appear out of nowhere whenever she found herself in a pickle—which was more often than not given her mischievous ways—and settle whatever dispute was ailing her.

Narena recalled a time when she couldn't have been more than ten.

She had wandered off from her home at the palace, which she was prone to do as she was often left to her own devices as a child, and stumbled upon a deer carcass rotting by a freshly fallen tree. Upon creeping toward it for a closer look, she was accosted by a very grumpy and very territorial turkey vulture. The vulture lunged at Narena, and she leaped backwards while slamming her eyes shut to avoid the sight of her own bloody demise. But just before the vulture tore into her young flesh, an arrow whizzed out of nowhere and sliced through the vulture's left eye. The beast howled in agony, and took off in an instant into the sky.

I never thanked him, Narena thought, as she remembered how she had stormed away in a huff, back to the palace, and told the king that Kellen had been following her. Nothing ever came of the incident after that.

"All right. Now that we've all rested and eaten, it's time we took off again," Nessaba's shrill voice interrupted Narena's thoughts.

"Now where are we going?" Nyxen asked.

"To Lapis Mountain," the witch replied. "I have my knapsack with all the supplies we'll need for the spell. Let's make haste!"

"Here we go again," Kellen muttered. But this time, rather than retort back at her old friend, Narena simply slipped her tiny, soft hand into his, looked him straight in the eye, and kissed him on the cheek.

"Let's go," she whispered. Kellen flushed pink, but did not resist in the slightest. So the two followed Nessaba, as she fluttered away in bat form, walking hand in hand from the witch's home, their friends following closely behind.

CHAPTER 14

"So, when's the wedding?" Sebillon asked after the group had walked for some time.

"What do you mean?" Narena replied.

"You and Kellen. Dating? Betrothed? What?"

"Nothing," Kellen snapped. "I've known this girl my whole life. What's it to you?"

"I'm just wondering. Obviously there's some kind of unspoken thing here," Sebillon grinned.

"Mind your own business," Kellen shot back.

"Don't mind him," Hawthorne said. "He's always like this. At least as long as I've known him, anyway."

"Okay, forget I asked." Sebillon took off and fluttered over to Nyxen. "What's his deal?" she asked, pointing her thumb in Kellen's direction.

"He's just overprotective of my sister," Nyxen explained quietly to Sebillon. "After our parents died, the king invited us to live at the palace with his family. Kellen's father is the General of Nymph Army, so he also spent a lot of time at the palace. We all kind of grew up together. I've even known Hawthorne since I was seven or so, but I'm not sure Kellen knew him as well as my sister and I did."

"And how long have your sister and Kellen had their weird thing?" Sebillon asked.

"As long as I can remember. Neither one will admit it, though. They pretend like they despise each other most of the time."

"Nyxen, can I ask another question?"

"Sure."

"Why did King Alston let you and your sister live at the palace? That seems awfully nice of him, and I was to understand that he was a real jerk."

"He didn't really have much of a choice, I guess. My parents died saving his life, during the war against the goblins. He promised he would raise us as a last request. I was only six at the time. Narena was eight."

"That's terrible. Nyxen, I'm so sorry." Nyxen looked into Sebillon's cerulean eyes and nodded.

Nyxen felt the goosebumps riddle his skin, and coughed awkwardly, hoping the faery would not take notice. He had always been one to act in a calm, collected manner around females, perhaps a tactic adopted from having such a headstrong sister, but found in this instance that he was no longer the practical, overly intelligent nymph he prided himself on being. Ever since he could remember, he had found most females to be immature, oblivious, and self-absorbed, but in the case of Sebillon, well, she simply made him weak at the knees. And if she did possess any of those qualities, which was very possible, Nyxen at this time was disinclined to notice.

"So Nessaba," Hawthorne asked the bat witch as the group continued walking. "What do we intend to do once we reach Lapis

Mountain? Is there any way we should prepare for facing Labete?"

"Not in the slightest, my dear," the witch replied, flapping above the group. "So long as you keep love in your hearts and good intentions in your mind, we shouldn't need any further training to stand against Labete. There have been battles waged on good by evil since the dawn of time, and this is no different."

"But it is!" Kellen protested. "This a Higher Spirit we're talking about!"

"Not only that," Narena continued. "But a Higher Spirit possessed by an Under Spirit. I've never read any Forest history that deals with something like this."

"Stop worrying your little heads," Nessaba said. "I'm not sure you are aware of the magnitude of powers you hold as a unit. But you'll find out soon enough."

"But how are we going to destroy a Higher Spirit?" Sebillon asked.

"Simple," Nessaba replied. "Only the Highest Spirit can destroy another Higher Spirit. We must awaken the Yew."

"That's definitely going to be a challenge," Narena said. "From what I understand, that's one of the hardest spells to perform. Does that mean we will have to sacrifice a life?"

"We'll cross that bridge when we get to it," Nessaba replied.

"Stop!" Kellen hissed, and shoved Narena behind a bush. Nessaba instantaneously dropped to the ground and helped him scoot the rest of the group out of sight.

"Ew, what is that?" Sebillon scoffed, and Narena delicately peeked around the bush to witness a horror of sights.

A black mass, thick and dark as the midnight twilight, was hovering over what appeared to be the carcass of a large animal. The mass pulsated as it slurped the corpse, shrinking the body until it was void of its insides. All that was left were the bones of the once-animal and a furry, leathery skin suit. In one swift movement, the mass boomed back into the corpse, filling the empty skin and cracking the skeleton back into form. Then the creature rose from the ground, and Narena was able to ascertain that it was once a mature bear, though it no longer resembled anything other than a monstrous beast.

The beast then roared a booming death scream and galloped off, away from the group and into the thickest, darkest part of the Forest.

"It's heading to Lapis Mountain," Nessaba whispered. "We must follow it, the creature holds the spirit of Labete inside it."

"Through the darkest part of the Forest?" Kellen groaned. "We don't even venture there for warrior training!"

"Well, we don't have much of a choice. It's the quickest way to the mountain," Nessaba replied.

"Everybody stay close," Narena said.

"I'll put a protective barrier around us," Hawthorne chimed in. He whispered an incantation to himself and swirled his hands around his body, creating a bluish fire that danced around him, and he flicked his hands around the whole group, engulfing it within the flames. "Don't step out of this barrier," he warned. "If you do, my magic can't help you."

The group nodded in reply and crept its way into the darkest part of the Forest. As they entered, the trees behind them seemed to close in on their heels, forming a wall that prevented them from turning back.

Here goes nothing, Narena thought, and walked with her friends into the darkness.

Chapter 15

The air in the darkest region of the forest loomed around the group in a thick fog that seemed to permeate through Hawthorne's protective barrier. It was like a blockade, a wall that enacted itself directly in front of the group at all times, prompting them to stop and explore the details of the harrowing place, but promising a sense of a torturous demise if any being were to comply.

The oak trees in this part of the Forest were a charcoal gray, and twisted from the trunks in an arthritic ensemble that crept from the drooping canopies to the blackened Forest floor. And while the good part of the Forest's floor was a reddish-orange from piles of old pine needles, fallen oak leaves, and strings of redwood bark, the darkest part of the Forest's floor was a thick, muddy, and stale ash-gray. Even the water of the creek, which was previously clear as a polished quartz crystal, now held a polluted, smoky clay color. Disembodied whoops and howls echoed through the woods, and all feelings of hopelessness and despair trickled through one's mind with every diabolical sight and sound.

"No wonder we never came in here," Kellen muttered to Narena. "This place is dire."

Narena nodded, but kept her eyes on some slight movement that she noticed beneath one of the smaller oak trees. Something resembling large, bulbous eyes was peeking out of the soil at her. Narena stopped, prompting the group to stop with her. She squinted, and focused her full attention upon the creature that appeared to be maneuvering itself out of the dirt.

"Look," she whispered. "Do you see that? It looks like a toad."

"Leave it alone," Nessaba hissed. "Nothing good can ever come out of this ground."

"What if he's stuck?" Narena whimpered. "We can help him get to the better part of the Forest."

"He's not stuck," Kellen said. "Now let's go."

Narena felt a pressure on her skull, as if an invisible finger was lightly tapping on her head. The eyes peering out of the ground blinked at her. "He needs help," she said in a voice unlike her own, appearing to be in some form of trance. "We have to help him."

"No. We. Don't," Nyxen hissed. "Narena, snap out of it!"

Help me, the toad implored in Narena's mind, and she now found herself gazing through still memories of times she had been helpless while witnessing innocent animals suffering. Age six, a drowning bee that was too far out-stream for her to rescue. Age eight, a robin that had slammed into a tree, breaking its neck. Age eleven, a gopher that had been crushed by a fallen tree limb. Age sixteen, a deer that had been shot in one of the adjoining woods near their Forest, and oh! How she would never forget that deer's death scream! The deer's scream resounded once more in her mind.

"I will!" she cried out. She burst herself through the protective flames, rushing toward the toad and frantically tearing at the earth around him.

"No! Narena! Stop!" Kellen called.

"Get back here!" Nyxen hissed, as did Sebillon and Hawthorne.

"She's too sensitive!" Nessaba wailed. "I knew this would be a problem at some point. Narena, get your little nymph butt back here!"

Narena ignored her friends and continued digging the helpless toad out of the ground. She grabbed the toad under his arms and attempted to pull him out, but found upon doing so that the creature would not budge. She pulled harder, and his body began to stretch like rubber, squeezing his eyeballs out of their sockets.

"Narena! It's not a real toad!" Hawthorne called out, and Narena turned her head to look at the salamander.

"He won't come out!" she said helplessly, only to witness her friends' eyes widen.

"Turn around!" Kellen shouted, and Narena obliged.

A heaving, writhing, slimy beast was drooling above her shoulders, peering its bloodshot eyes down into her soul. Narena screamed, slapped her hand over her mouth, and slammed her eyes shut.

"It's not a toad," she whimpered, and started blindly backing away. "Help…"

"Open your eyes, Narena!" Nyxen called exasperatedly. "She always does this," he hissed to the group. "I don't know why she always shuts her eyes!"

Narena continued backing away, eyes closed, body trembling. She knew what stood before her, ready to destroy any being of light that disturbed it, but she simply refused to believe that the innocent toad was actually a deceiving dark entity.

Please, she implored within her mind. Please, I am a pure soul. I just wanted to help.

In her mind, Narena saw an image of a warty toad that resembled the one who had just transformed. Its aura was one of light, and she was able to ascertain that this entity had overtaken the toad at some point, and it was not inherently bad. She opened her eyes, but saw to her dismay that it was indeed still the entity who was heaving before her.

The entity snarled, and loomed down over the small nymph. Narena squeezed her eyes shut again and held her hand over her blade. Then her demeanor changed, and she began to feel the warrior inside of her start to creep its way out.

Dare mess with me, dark entity, Narena thought, and you're going to find yourself in a world of trouble.

Such big words for such a small, insignificant being, the entity projected into her mind. If you can't even pass by me without meddling, how do you expect to destroy Labete?

Narena opened her eyes to find that the entity was pulling itself back to take a cheap shot at her. She thought about shutting her eyes again and waiting for the blow, but instead clenched her teeth and swung her arm up, blade in hand, and jammed it across the entity's third eye, just barely grazing it. But that was enough to throw the entity a fox tail's length backward, and allow her to ready her position once more.

The entity pulled back again and shot itself straight at Narena, howling as it traveled the mere second before reaching her body. Narena ducked into a fetal position and swung her blade around blindly in the air. She prepared herself for the impact, but when it didn't happen right away, she cautiously looked out to witness Kellen doing what he did best.

Kellen leaped through the protective fire and dashed toward Narena, firing an arrow directly at the beast's face. It sliced across the top of its eye and the beast howled, shaking its head around and spitting in all directions. Kellen grabbed Narena's arm and dragged her stiff body back to the group, shooting another arrow into the beast's chest before Hawthorne quickly re-enacted the protective barrier, and the group sprinted and flew away.

"I'm so sorry," Narena said when they had finally gotten far enough to speak.

"Don't worry about it," Kellen grunted. "You're not trained for this kind of stuff, I can't expect you to act as if you were."

"Just don't do anything like that ever again, okay?" Nyxen said. "I'm not so keen on being an only child. Seems like a lonely existence... no offense Kellen."

"I... I just don't know what came over me," Narena replied. "That... that thing... played on my sympathy. I felt bad for it, and it took advantage of that."

"Of course it did," Nessaba said. "Have you forgotten where you are? This whole section of the Forest thrives on deception and negativity. The Under Spirits rule as much here as they do the underworld. And you, Narena, are too sensitive. You need to learn how to psychically protect yourself. Otherwise, your sensitivity will prove you a curse, when it should be a blessing."

"I'm sure at some point that creature was a real toad," Hawthorne said softly. "It was probably influenced by something evil."

"Yes, this area is much worse than I remember," Nessaba said. "We must power through as quickly as possible."

"Looks like we don't have much of a choice in that," Nyxen gulped, and the group turned to him to see he was staring wide-eyed at something behind them.

The group turned around simultaneously, only to find a massive gathering of dark shadows, varying in size, shape, and depth of color, looming around in the path behind them.

"What are those?" Sebillon asked, her voice shaky.

"Entities," Nessaba replied. "And creatures of darkness."

The shadows heaved around and started to lurch closer. Narena was able to make out several entities and creatures she recognized from her books, and quickly pointed each one out to the group.

"There's another kalpie on the right, three or four goblins in the middle there, a greed spirit, the hunger spirit, the suffering spirit... and there's that swarm of insects that ate the mousey creature..."

Kellen grabbed Narena's arm. "Now is not the time for..."

"Um, shouldn't we go?" Nyxen asked hurriedly.

"On my word, turn and go as fast as you possibly can. Do not look back. And do not stop until I say so," Nessaba hissed. "Ready... one, two, three, *GO!*"

Narena turned and took off, with the group beside and flying above her, seeing only a tunnel of blurred gray-scale through the passing darkness around her and, in her peripherals, the tanned outline of Kellen running directly at her side.

CHAPTER 16

As the group traveled toward Lapis Mountain, far away from Nymph Kingdom, back at the palace King Alston was on a quest of his own. His attempts to contact his teacher were futile, and upon realizing he would not reach Labete, the king decided to take matters into his own hands.

Alston sat at his desk in his library, his head in his hands, knowing well what was expected of him as a ruler, and yet he was reluctant to go through with it.

Awkening the Yew, he thought to himself. Why is it so difficult to bring myself to do it?

"Honey?" Alston's thoughts were interrupted by the sweet, cooing voice of his beloved wife, Tiatana. Her long, golden locks hung in wisps around her lovely face, and Alston peered up at her, realizing she must have whisked herself into the room unnoticed.

"Yes, my dear?" he replied.

"Felide wishes to meet with you, are you completely swamped with work?”

"I suppose not. Tell him I will be in the throne room momentarily." Tiatana nodded, smiled, and backed out of the room.

Alston turned back to his desk and sighed. *So much for the spell for now.*

Waking the Yew was no minor nymph matter, or any matter for the beings of the Forest, in that sense. King Alston's very crown was on the line, and if the Yew was wakened and felt as though it was not merited, Alston would surely be stripped of his crown and title, and who knows, perhaps find himself in a similar predicament as the very Spirit that had caused him such grief in the first place—Labete.

But King Alston was by no means humble. In fact, his crown was often questioned as his decisions regarding Nymph Kingdom were often considered rash and unwarranted to the good of the community, but the oblivious nature of nymphs did not incline the beings to take any form of action or protest against him, at least not outwardly. Perhaps he too was partially at fault for the falling that was in the process of occurring.

A being's ego, however large or small, though not roughly correlated with the actual size of a being's stature, was known to have extreme, unrealized power. Power fully capable of twisting a normal mind frame to one of negativity. Acknowledging one's ego can be helpful to one's spiritual progress, though ignorance toward it surely led to one's demise. Alston was aware of this, but still had always chosen the needs of his own first. Until his recent loss of his son, that is.

Alston's thoughts now turned to his son, and he recalled when Rowan was born. He had given Tiatana a difficult and drawn out labor, but he finally emerged, a mass of golden yellow hair surrounding a tiny, pink little face. Rowan was born looking like a lion, and Alston could remember thinking that he had every pinch of royal blood apparent at birth. He would have been a perfect king. Better than himself, even. But now, what of now? A relationship torn apart by the falling, like so many others.

Alston couldn't help but feel resentment that a Spirit he trusted would betray not only him, but all of his people, and simultaneously put every being in the Forest at grave risk. He had been deceived, but he was not of negative influence enough to forget the love of his family.

"Rowan," he couldn't help but whisper. He sighed as his mind slid through mental pictures of times he shared with his only child, and found himself becoming more and more angry at Labete.

How dare he! Alston clenched his teeth. After he trained me! Took me under his wing for years, taught me everything I needed to know to be a good leader! He didn't prepare me for this in any form, and especially without my heir to pass the knowledge along!

"You're never going to solve anything if you just sit around here and mope," a sniveling, husky-sounding voice spoke. Alston jolted up and found himself staring directly into his very own sea-blue eyes. But it was not a doppelganger of the king, but rather his son, Rowan, who was standing before him.

"Rowan," Alston said. "But it can't be... I was sure you had perished."

Alston panicked in his mind when he realized he hadn't adequately searched for his son to the full extent he could have. Sure, he had sent out a team of warriors to look, but made sure they didn't venture into the darker parts of the Forest, where more of his own kind could be lost to the darkness. If Rowan had been in there, the king had said to Felide, he is perished as we know it. The search team returned after just a couple of days of looking to no avail.

"I did perish, Father. This is me without the burden of my physical body."

"I do not believe in ghosts. Either you went up or went down. Which is it?"

"You had better start believing in ghosts. Your ignorance to the spiritual world will never help your Forest. You're a walking contradiction. A hypocrite, if you will."

"Rowan, what happened to you?" Alston ignored Rowan's comment.

"I was taken. Taken by the darkness. Labete now has control of my sense of will, and can bid my spirit to perform his bidding. But there is still some good in me, Father, enough good to allow me to show you the best of what is left of my spirit before that good dies completely, which it inevitably will. I can project myself to be perceived by you in any way that I want. But before I am gone forever, I wanted to say my final goodbyes, since it was from you that I have learned everything I know. How to behave, how to feel, how to react... and how to never give up on what you want.

"If Labete is destroyed, any manifestation of myself is likely to be gone forever. From what I gather, any being attached to him will cease to exist. But the evil energy in me is growing strong as I become more resentful of my fate. I do not desire to fight for Labete, I wish only to rely on myself! But I am bound to him... because of you."

Alston could no longer hide his guilt, whether it be for his son, or more likely, for himself. Tears began to stream from his cerulean eyes.

"Please Rowan, how can I help? What can I do?"

"Nothing more than you have already started. Perform your spell, Father. I want you to awaken the Yew. I spent so much of my life being pompous and selfish, and I realize now that it is all meaningless if this is how I am to be. If not for the good of the Forest, avenge me to Labete. Awaken the Yew and destroy him!"

Rowan opened his mouth and roared a booming sound as the gleam of his image faded, and finally his whole manifestation. Alston fell to his knees, sobbing, calling for his son. But Rowan was gone, the only trace of him now being the memory of his piercing eyes in Alston's mind.

After a few minutes of grieving his child, Alston picked himself up with the realization that if he could not save Rowan, he must perform Rowan's final wishes. Alston's pride would not allow him to not attempt to avenge his son. He knew that the spell he was about to perform would make the whole Forest take notice. Performing this spell would also cause Labete to no doubt try to influence as many beings to his side as he possibly could, in addition, of course, to sending out the dark entities he knew and had since transformed. Alston needed every angle to be in favor of him and his kind.

Alston rushed to his throne room, where Felide, Tiatana, and Chancellor Lyren were awaiting him, and the looks on their faces conveyed that they knew what he was about to decree.

"Lyren, send off the Forest signal. All warriors are called to report. We are declaring war on Labete."

"Yes, your Highness. And may I comment, it's about time," Lyren replied. Felide said nothing, but his face spoke an anthology of emotions.

"I care not for your comments. Now I demand solitude in the library until I emerge of my own accord. Felide will lead this war, as I have a very important task at hand."

Lyren simply nodded and walked briskly out of the room. Felide shook hands with the king and left, and Tiatana gave him a light kiss on the cheek.

"This isn't your fault," she said softly.

"Whether it is or not, I now plan to take responsibility for it," the king replied, turned away, and sauntered back to the library. Now all he needed was to find the book with the spell, and he could begin the process of awakening the Yew.

CHAPTER 17

The group had nearly reached the end of the darkest part of the Forest, but the looming entities had not yet given up on stalking their every move. Though the entities had not attacked nor addressed the group in the slightest, their presence continued to be a thickness of tension that affected every step taken in the protective barrier.

A light shooting through the thick trees became brighter and brighter as the group approached a brief clearing. Behind it lied what looked like a huge brownish-gray rock, and as they got closer they noticed it was not one rock, but actually the base of an enormous mountain, with scattered trees and bushes glittering its base, and jagged rocks resembling stalactites shoving out of the mountain's side. It was almost as if the jagged rocks were trying to leap off the side of the mountain, seemingly trying to escape the thick, tense energy that oozed from the very top like a volcano. Above it, the sky surrounding the top appeared much darker in comparison to every other direction around the mountain, and was colored by a stale grayish-periwinkle.

"We're here," Narena whispered, as the group stepped over their last line of darkened Forest floor. "Lapis Mountain."

"Indeed we are," Nessaba said, peering behind her for one last glimpse of the glowing eyes and darting shadows that wailed in disappointment of lost victims. "We're safe... for now."

"Can we rest for a moment?" Nyxen asked. "My head is pounding. The trees in that last bit of Forest were ruthless in trying to contact me. Said pretty terrible things too, and their insults only got worse when I told them to leave me alone."

"What did they say to you?" Narena asked.

"Awful stuff. Stuff about our parents. They taunt you with your fears and insecurities, and then feed off it. Can we please stop for a bit?"

"We can rest, certainly, but not here. We should get up the mountain's side a least a little bit. I'm wary of resting near all our new friends," Nessaba said, motioning to the Forest behind her.

The group agreed and continued onwards, up a fairly less rugged summit of the mountain's side. Once they had reached a far enough away point where they could no longer see into the Forest anymore, they decided to stop and rest.

"You okay, Nyxen?" Narena asked as they sat down.

"I'm all right. Headache is slowly going away."

"So do you remember what those dark trees said to you?"

"Why do you want to know?"

"I'm just curious. If what they said are my fears too, isn't it better to acknowledge them?"

"If you must know," Nyxen muttered. "They said it was our fault they died. And how we got to spend our childhoods in luxury so we were probably happy about them dying, and we only helped Alston be who he is."

Narena gasped. "Wow. That's definitely what I used to think that the rest of the kingdom thought about me."

"Nobody thought that," Kellen said to Narena's surprise. She had assumed he hadn't been listening, as he was sharpening his blade on a rock a few fox tail's lengths away. "If anything, everyone felt bad for you. Nobody would want that for themselves."

"I can't believe they'd say something like that to you!" Sebillon broke in, putting her hand on Nyxen's forearm. "What jerks."

"Did you just call those trees 'jerks'?" Nyxen asked, laughing. "I have to say, that's pretty funny."

"You know, the more I think about it," Narena said, "the more I seem to remember Mother getting headaches a lot. I remember feeling slighted when it would prevent her from spending time with me, exploring."

"Guess we know why now, huh?" Nyxen replied. "And I finally sympathize with how many naps she used to take during the day. Hearing the trees is exhausting!"

"I bet," Narena said. "And that mixed with how rambunctious we were! No wonder she napped all the time."

"She didn't have a mean bone in her body," Kellen chimed in from across the way. "She was always very kind to me, even when my acornball broke one of her stained-glass windows. And she was an amazing mother indeed, to put up with you two."

"What about your mother, Kellen?" Sebillon called back. "Was she a tree whisperer, too?"

"No," Kellen replied curtly. "She wasn't."

"But she was a very special nymph, nonetheless," Narena chimed in.

"I'd rather not discuss her," Kellen said, getting up from his seat and starting to walk away. "Shouldn't we be going?"

"We have a few more moments of rest," Nessaba said. "I think we should replenish all we can now, while we still can. I'm not sure if we'll have opportunities for rest once we climb higher."

"Perfect! Then you can answer my question!" Sebillon declared. "Why are you so walled up, Kellen? I feel like I'm getting to know everyone here except you."

"And I'd like to keep it that way," Kellen snapped, and started walking off. "Why don't you enlighten us with some faery tales instead?" He stormed around the side of a boulder, out of sight.

"That probably is best," Narena said. Her voice dropped to a whisper. "And Sebillon, I think you should drop the mother talk around him."

"Why?" Sebillon asked.

"Kellen's mother died. Freak accident, really. It happened when I was about ten. Kellen would have been in his late teens. I think it was right around the time he graduated from studies and enrolled in warrior training. So yes, he would have been seventeen or so."

"What kind of accident?"

"Um, I guess it was more of an attack. Being in the wrong place at the wrong time."

"Attack by what?"

"Kalpie."

Sebillon slapped her hand over her mouth. "That's awful! So she drowned, then?"

"Yeah," Narena gulped the lump in her throat. "I already made the mistake of mentioning it to him before we met you, so it's probably a good idea not to bring it up again. And that was right before we encountered one and he nearly tore the creature to shreds, so I know he still has a lot of pent-up emotion about the whole thing."

"Wow, well I definitely won't bring it up again. But one more thing if you don't mind."

"Sure."

"So then Kellen's mother was the nymph who prompted the kingdoms pushing the kalpies to the outskirts of the Forest?"

"Yep. Well, the ones that Alston didn't have killed first."

"Wow, I feel terrible. Next time I try to pry too much, stop me, okay?"

Narena smiled. "Okay."

Narena had never prided herself on being a good friend to females, so this new friendship that seemed to be blossoming among herself and Sebillon was a pleasant surprise. This was the first time that she could even recall a female even taking the slightest interest in her as a friend, without Narena having to instigate a seemingly forced interaction.

Back in her younger years, Narena usually had only one good female friend at a time, as she found it near impossible to maintain two, let alone an entire group of female friends. Most of the female friendships that Narena was able to secure ended up being short-lived, as her obliviousness always prompted her to say something awkward, or innocently insulting to the girl without even realizing it. She would just get so anxious and eager to please that she would simply blurt out things that sounded nice in her mind but didn't always sound the way she meant aloud. These comments would add up in the friend's mind, and eventually they would grow tired of her feeble attempts to be one of the girls, and fade away just like all the others.

"All right, my little ones," Nessaba's voice broke in. "Time to move on."

"Not for me," Hawthorne said. "I think this is where my journey ends."

"What?!" Narena cried, rushing to her friend. "Why?!"

"I'm an amphibian," he replied. "The higher I climb, the more oxygen I lose. If I go any higher I'll die. I'm sure of it."

"Then you should stay," Kellen declared. "You can be our lookout from below."

"Very well. I should be able to implant thoughts to your minds through meditation from here, in case I need to warn you of any impending adversaries. Narena, I think you're the strongest intuitive of the group. Be open for my messages."

Narena's eyes filled with tears as Hawthorne's dismissal from the group became more real to her. She panicked within her mind at the thought of losing her good friend. But again, she felt Kellen's rough, warm hand on the small of her back, and sighed deeply.

"Goodbye, my dear friend," she said as she embraced Hawthorne. "I will see you soon, whether alive or in the afterlife!"

"It better be alive," Hawthorne replied with a smile. "Take care of her," he said to Kellen as he shook his hand. "If she doesn't come back, I'm coming after you! Don't forget, I know where you live."

"I will," Kellen replied. "And she will come back. Even if I don't, I'll make sure that she does."

The group finished saying their goodbyes to Hawthorne and took off once again on the path up the side of the mountain. Narena only looked back once, only to find that her salamander friend was meditating peacefully on a dewy leaf, swirls of fire dancing around his body as he transcended.

"Goodbye…" she whispered again, and turned to catch up with Kellen at the front of the group.

"You gonna be okay?" Kellen asked softly, slipping his hand into hers.

"I'll be fine," Narena replied. "There's not much choice in the matter, anyway."

"You're strong on your own, you know," Kellen said. "You don't need to always stand behind someone to protect you. You're a powerful girl, and I've always known that. It's one of my favorite attributes of yours."

"Thanks Kellen. That means a lot, especially coming from you."

"I'm serious!"

"I know, I'm just teasing."

"That's another thing I like. Your sense of humor."

"Yeah, I'm almost as morbid as you."

"I prefer macabre to morbid."

Narena laughed. "Of course you would."

"Shh," Nessaba broke in. "From this point on, no more speaking. When we reach the summit we can figure out how to proceed."

The small beings nodded in acquiescence and continued trudging up the side of Lapis Mountain, further away from their Forest, and deeper into the unknown.

Chapter 18

ack in the Forest, the sacred clearing began to fill with a myriad of Forest dwellers, mostly warriors of various species, called together for a common purpose. Nymphs, faeries, cardinals, blue jays, owls, trolls, gnomes, squirrels, rabbits, toads, foxes, deer, and even a few snakes made up the congregation, each equipped with a weapon of their own device. Arrows, blades, shields, teeth, claws, beaks, talons, tails, speed, and intelligence all stood opposition to Labete's indiscretions. And right in the center of it all stood Felide, General of Nymph Army, upon a tall, cylindrical rock, addressing the crowd.

"My friends and comrades, the time has come to end this falling. Too long has the Forest been plagued with fear. Labete has poisoned minds, violated the innocent, and persecuted the good for too long! It is time to fight back! If we perish, we will do so in fighting for good, reaching for the light. Be strong and do not forget what it is you are fighting for!"

The crowd roared in response as Felide hopped off the rock and began to lead the way toward Lapis Mountain, to the darkest part of the

Forest. This is where he knew Labete's dark entities to be hiding, waiting for his arrival, having the advantage of their known part of the Forest to ambush them within.

What a disgrace to lay in wait for us to come to the darkness to fight, Felide thought. I cannot wait to avenge Rowan's death upon these cowards.

Felide knew the nature of these dark beings well, and had never known them to play fair. He had, for the longest time, believed witches to be the only beings who could control or destroy negative entities, but after many years had discovered that in the right mindset, any being could manipulate the energies enough to have an affect on these dark beings.

Or just hit them square between the eyes, Felide thought, and chuckled to himself as he recalled an instance he had told his son about recently.

It was a time when the falling was first beginning, but not spoken of at all within the good parts of the Forest. But it was felt, certainly, by Felide himself and most others, but fear of repercussions from the king prevented most from mentioning it. During this time, one dark entity referred to as The Second, who was an accomplice and supporter of Labete likely sent to the Forest by Agrimon, took it upon himself to attack a traveling pair of faeries who were trying to deliver a message from their king, Laurel.

The note shared King Laurel's disapproval of Labete's rapid acquisition of power and demanded that all beings, royal or not, ground themselves and equalize their energies through whole kingdom meditations, which would regain the balance necessary for the Forest to continue in harmony.

But King Alston, of course, ignored the message and delayed a response from Nymph Kingdom, likely because he did not want to equalize his energy with common folk, so the time deferred allowed Labete enough time to find out the message. This did not sit well with Labete, who most likely found out by way of divination, and it was unclear if Labete sent The Second out to perform this attack or he did it of his own accord. Either way, the faery messengers were attacked, consumed by darkness, and presumably perished.

A short time later the Faery King was rumored to have been visited by the spirits of these messengers, who warned him to stop Labete before the situation got worse. This prompted the Faery King to reach out to King Alston, who scoffed at the idea, but still sent Felide and ten warriors to the Faery Kingdom to appease the Faery King.

It was there that Felide had an encounter with The Second, as the entity saw the faeries now as a weak species and had returned to finish off the whole kingdom. But as the nymphs and faeries were attacked, Felide discovered by accident that a perfectly placed arrow shot between the eyes and slightly above the eyebrow line perished The Second, who relied on his third eye to even exist, let alone attack, in the realm to which the Forest resided.

It was these accidental discoveries that always seemed to give Felide an extra edge on the opposition, and ultimately, what made him such an accomplished warrior. His instinct was true, and always trusted, as past experiences had taught. Felide felt himself feeling more ready for the inevitable battle that was to come, and he only hoped that his sentiment would carry over to the strangest species combination army he had ever led into battle.

"Um, excuse me, General?" A sharp voice permeated Felide's mind. "Might I have a word?"

Felide looked to his right and found a red fox with chestnut brown eyes strutting beside him as he walked. "Yes, what can I do for you?"

"Do you remember me?" the fox asked. "I know it was a long time ago, but I remember it like it was yesterday... must have been three or four litters of puppies ago for me."

Felide squinted his eyes. "Virgil?" he asked, his thoughts playing through images of his past encounters with foxes. He could only recall one that was fairly significant in his mind.

"Yes! You remember!" The fox panted, with drool dripping down the sides of his mouth. "If not for you, I'd still be stuck in that sinkhole over by the creek! I owe you my freedom... no, my life!"

"Don't worry about it," Felide replied with a smile.

"You were kind to me when you didn't know me, and I am much bigger than you. I could have turned around and bitten your head right off!" Virgil laughed, and in one swift movement of his jaws, picked up Felide by the belt and swung him around onto his back. "For that, Felide, I would follow you straight into the depths of darkness!"

"Watch your tongue, my fox friend, for that is just what we are about to do."

Felide focused his eyes on the path ahead, as the speed of travel had propelled him to where he could now see the end of light in the Forest. Beyond that, though he knew the Forest continued, there was only darkness.

Within that darkness, Felide could see varying depths of blackness darting around among the twisting tree branches, sometimes joined by reflective duos of red lights.

Eyes. Watching us approach.

Felide knew this battle was the one that every other experience in his life had led him up to. This was no simulation. This wasn't a simple dispute within species, or a conflict resolution of a rash decree or decision, or even just one entity to fight. Only a Higher Spirit could help this end, and Felide wondered at this point if any would even be willing to help.

Alston better be awakening that Yew, Felide thought, as he motioned to his army. Then, with one throw of his arm, Felide gave the word and the army charged straight into the darkness.

Chapter 19

Much time had passed since the group had continued on without Hawthorne, and it had finally reached the summit of Lapis Mountain. Nessaba and Kellen poked around, scoping out the area for any potential threats before motioning for the group to gather up.

"Okay, my little ones, the coast is clear enough for us to rest up for a bit," Nessaba declared. "After we have all rested up we will continue on, into a cave that I saw just a couple hundred fox tail's lengths away from where we are now."

"I'll keep watch," Kellen said, "while the rest of you can sleep."

The group agreed on the plan, and began to make themselves comfortable on the rough terrain. Though sleep did not readily evade them, as they were exhausted from all their travels. Nyxen, Sebillon, and Narena had no trouble falling asleep right away, but it was Narena who found herself plagued with a harsher reality existing within her subconscious.

In her dream, Narena found herself sitting cross legged in a cave, presumably one that was attached to the very mountain she was currently resting upon. She got the distinct impression that it was late in the night, despite the sun glaring on her sleeping face.

The cave was dark, not even the smallest glare of the moon penetrated the deep shadows to which Narena found her eyes gazing upon. In the short distance, she could make out a form twitching within the shadows, a black form only so much darker than the depth of shadows surrounding it. It was massive, and the only distinguishing feature Narena could make out were two glowing yellow eyes. The form loomed over her, freezing her in place, demanding acquiescence to its presence yet not allowing Narena the free will to acknowledge it by her own purpose. Her mouth opened to speak yet no words escaped her throat.

The entity gazed at her, penetrating her soul with not just its eyes, but its mere presence as well. Narena was unable to do anything but gaze back, and hope whatever this was would release its grasp upon her. Time seemed to stop, and yet go on for an eternity. Finally, Narena heard words spoken directly into her mind, in a deep, raspy voice, almost like a growl.

You must help me, the voice spoke. Narena panicked within her mind, as she feared any thought would be transmitted to the entity. She chose her thoughts wisely.

I do not know what it is you want from me, and your approach is not one of needing assistance, rather one of intimidation. How do I know you are speaking the truth?

I was once a good spirit, Narena. The darkness has consumed me. Everything I once was has been masticated into what I appear before you. I fear I cannot be helped.

Are you Labete?

I suppose I am the subconscious of Labete's last hope as a mortal. If you exorcise this darkness in the right way I may be spared, but I'm afraid it may be at cost to you. If I am freed of this I will be of great importance to the future of the Forest.

I do not know of what cost you speak, but had you not made a significant mark upon the Forest, I would not be here in the first place. I am greatly sympathetic as far as beings go, though I am not sure I can harbor much sympathy for you, Sir.

In life there are always different paths that can be chosen. The choices you make about how you destroy me, or send me to salvation, whichever you choose, will have a profound effect upon the Forest. But rest assured, my little friend, that King Alston will handle you appropriately whichever path you choose.

And with that, the entity released its grasp on Narena, and dissipated into the air in a burst of gray smoke.

Narena jilted awake, shaken by her dream, and found that Kellen was standing over her, peering down at her distraught, sweat-soaked face.

"Another bad dream?" he asked.

"You have no idea," Narena replied, getting up and brushing herself off. "How long was I out for?"

"Just an hour or so. I was just about to wake everyone else up." Kellen walked over to Nyxen and Sebillon and gave each of them a tender shake of the shoulders. They, too, stood up and stretched.

"Are we ready to head off again?" Nessaba said. "Good. I've given Kellen instructions on where to find Labete, so follow him through the cave and obey his every command. This is where I'll leave you."

"Oh no!" Narena cried. "Not you too!"

"Why are you leaving us?" Nyxen asked.

"I'm afraid I have to. Somebody has to perform the spell to awaken the Yew. I'll cast my circle out here, where I can see better and have more space. It will also be easier to reach the Yew from out here than it would be deep in the depths of the cave, and I'd bet that Labete has some kind of hex on the cave to prevent the spell from being performed in there anyway."

"What will we do without you?" Narena lamented.

Nessaba chuckled. "You'll be fine. I have complete faith in all of you."

"Come on, we'd better get going," Kellen broke in. "The sun is starting to set."

Narena approached Nessaba and wrapped her little arms around one of her ankles, burying her face in her sock. "I'll miss you, Nessaba."

Nessaba peered down. "I'll miss you too. It's been lovely getting to know you these past few days. Please, Narena, promise me that you'll trust in yourself?"

Narena's eyes swelled with tears. "I'll try."

"I don't want you to try. I want you to do."

"I will."

"That's better. Now, get out of here. I need to begin my spell."

Kellen reached out his hand. "Come on, Narena, we need to go."

Narena took Kellen's hand and allowed him to lead her away from Nessaba and toward the cave, with Nyxen and Sebillon closely behind. When they had reached the mouth of the cave, the group stopped and all took in a deep breath.

Narena handed out candles from her knapsack to her brother and Kellen, who lit them and held them into the cave, swerving them back and forth to see into the depths of blackness that was about to surround them.

"Are we all ready?" Kellen asked as he took his first step into the darkened crevice. "Follow me, and stay close. If I stop, you stop. If I ready my weapon, ready yours."

Narena, Nyxen, and Sebillon all nodded. And, with the tiniest patter of little nymph feet, and the slightest flutter of wings, the group ventured into the darkness.

Hawthorne stood upright on a rock that overlooked the trail that the group had followed up the mountain, at the mouth of a small, moist crevice. His bulbous eyeballs peered around in front of him.

"I could have sworn I just heard something," he muttered to himself.

Though his eyesight was not nearly as sharp as a flying bird's, or even a small rodent for that matter, he still did his best to scan the skyline and trees below for any sign of an imposing threat. He had been meditating for quite some time, something that replenished his energy and enhanced his seeing abilities all his life. But suddenly, he awoke with a horrible, unsettling feeling, one that he simply could not shake out of his salamander mind, and the strange sound did not help matters. He was a sensitive of course, always had been, and his powers certainly were never something to be ignored.

Even when he was a young tadpole, so new to the world and yet so susceptible to danger, Hawthorne would take risks that no intelligent or experienced amphibian would. He was known to swim right up to the enormous, always cranky bullfrogs who, as ambush predators with no patience for nonsense or any disturbance of that matter, poke them square in the nose with the small, flailing arms he had begun to grow, and swim off as fast as possible, as the bullfrogs groaned and thrashed around, irritated at the joke but also at missing out on a tender, young meal.

How had I survived that? Either I was extremely cunning or extremely lucky. Probably the latter. He chuckled to himself.

But his amusement was quickly snapped away as he realized that his daydreaming had created quite the distraction.

The bad feeling. The sound. Keep watch. His mental reminders had always helped.

Hawthorne knew the quickest way to obtain the information of what was wrong was to meditate again, but he feared that if he took his concentration away from his guard for one moment it could be his very last.

And then what would become of my poor comrades? They'd end up like the rest of my kind. Influenced to the darkness or worse... death.

Not that Hawthorne harbored any doubts about the outcome of their quest, but that it seemed as though fear was finally beginning to seep its way into his once very well-protected mind.

Questioning oneself is certainly the first step, he thought, but was interrupted by a rustling in the trees below. He squinted his eyes and peered downwards.

His ears were keen, and able to pick up on the sound vibrations, making for better depth and length accuracy. Whatever was creating this rustling seemed to be small, although if the rustler in question was a spirit, who was to know the true magnitude of it. It could sound small, but in fact would have the capacity to appear much larger, and who even knew how strong it would be.

The fear swept over his small salamander body again. Full body chills. And not the chills of confirmation that he often got when asking a question of the universe. These were in fact fear chills, as Hawthorne had only experienced these one other time. A time he would not ever forget in his lifetime.

It was when he had narrowly escaped a swooping robin who, desperate for a meal during the beginning part of the falling, had mistaken poor Hawthorne for a tasty worm, in all the robin's starvation and delusions that had been caused by the falling. Luckily, he had paid attention to his feeling and ducked under a log just in time. These fear chills were not to be ignored.

Again, the rustle. This time closer, perhaps thirty human feet from Hawthorne's crevice.

How had this being moved so quickly? Either it was an animal morphologically equipped to handle such terrain or it was a being not of this physical world.

Hawthorne felt his heart rate rise. The beating pounded in his ribcage, so intensely that his delicate salamander ribs throbbed. The rustle again. This time, less than ten feet away.

Oh no, he thought. He had assumed he had a little more time. He looked at all directions at the entrance to the cave.

A gray mist floated into his direct eye line. His heart pounded faster.

The mist had seemingly no form, and was a musty shade of gray. It was currently about the size of a blooming sunflower, and it vibrated with a husky energy, almost quietly moaning. It floated directly in front of Hawthorne for a moment, appearing as though it was looking him over or sizing him up. Hawthorne felt a tingle in his mind and did all he could to shield himself from the being attempting to read his mind, or even steal his energy, possibly taking his life force.

But as quickly as the being arrived, it then darted upwards, seeming as though it felt Hawthorne was no threat, or had other business to deal with. Whatever reason it was, the entity left and Hawthorne sighed with relief, but his relaxation was short-lived when he realized who the entity was likely leaving to go after. He rushed to his meditation spot and the flames began to swirl around him as he desperately reached out mentally to warn his friends.

CHAPTER 20

The group moved deeper into the cave, and quickly found that the light which shone through the entrance was no longer visible. Now there was only the faint, flickering light of the candles, and all found it very difficult to see.

"Where is Labete?" Sebillon whispered. "How deep is he hiding?"

"I'm not quite sure," Kellen replied. "But Nessaba instructed me to just lead us forward through the cave, as deep as we're able to go."

"What are we supposed to do when we find him, anyway?" Nyxen asked quietly. "I don't know about you guys, but I've never gone against a Higher Spirit."

"Well, that's the problem," Narena spoke up. "I'm not sure we can. Everything I've read says that only another Higher Spirit can destroy one."

"Nessaba just wants us to hold Labete off while she completes the spell to awaken the Yew," Kellen replied. "And don't worry, I know what to do."

"What?" Nyxen asked.

"Hitting it in its third eye. For an entity, you can destroy it that way.

For a Higher or Under Spirit, it would weaken them. Enough so that they'd need to return to their dwellings in order to replenish their energy, giving you enough time to get away I guess."

"How do you know this?" Narena said. "I don't think I've ever read that."

"My father taught me. It's worked for him a couple times."

"Well, that's good to know."

Narena, a familiar voice spoke in Narena's mind. Narena, watch out! An entity is coming!

Narena froze. She caught a glimpse of some slight shadowy movement in the corner of her eye. Her heart began to race.

"Kellen..." she trailed off, poking him in the arm.

"Yeah?"

Narena gulped. "Look to your right."

Kellen turned his head, and saw what Narena was staring at.

"Ready your weapons," he said through clenched teeth. "Fire on my command. Aim for the forehead, right between the eyes."

The shadow shifted, and Narena could make out a misty shape, vibrating about in the flickering candlelight. Toward the top of the mass glared two piercing red eyes, and as Narena looked at them, they seemed to emit heat in her direction.

Kellen stepped slightly ahead of his friends, and readied his aim. "On my word..."

The red eyes swept from one being to another, finally fixated on Kellen, and laughed aloud.

"Stupid little creatures! You think you can defeat Labete? Try destroying Labete and Agrimon together, fused as one to create the Supreme Spirit! Most powerful of all! And the best part is, there is no longer any light within him! He only knows evil now, and soon you will all feel his wrath!"

"You're wrong!" Narena cried. "Evil can never win! Without good, there is no evil! And if Labete needs to be destroyed in order to defeat Agrimon and save the Forest, so be it! You don't scare us!"

"Naive little girl. You don't know what fear is! But you certainly will soon!"

The mass lurched backwards, and in one swift movement, shot itself at the group. Kellen fired an arrow, which sliced through the mass and slowed it down for a mere second. But the mass quickly countered back, hitting Kellen in the shoulder and knocking him over.

Narena rushed to Kellen to block his body as the mass looped around to strike Kellen again. She swung her blade in the direction of its third eye and just narrowly missed hitting it directly. She did manage to graze the side of it, sufficiently irritating the entity and causing it to swing down at her several times. But Narena kept slicing through the air at the mass, and it finally whooshed itself up to the ceiling of the cave.

Sebillon wasted no time in firing an arrow at the mass as it swooped around to shoot itself back at Narena again. Sebillon's arrow sliced into the mass's left eye, and it let out a bloodcurdling wail as it soared backward a few feet, then shot itself again at Sebillon, who was panicking as she tried to reload her bow. The mass screamed as it traveled at an unbelievable speed toward her, but just as it was about to smash its darkness into the small faery, Nyxen flew out of nowhere and stabbed the mass square between the eyes.

The entity roared, and tossed Nyxen's body against the wall of the crevice, causing a crunching sound, and a *THUD* as his limp body fell to the ground. The mass swirled and wailed, as if it could feel pain, and finally stopped mid-air, looked directly into Narena's wide, orange eyes, and burst into flames, the ashes quickly dropping to the floor and hissing as they absorbed into nothingness.

"Is everyone all right?" Kellen asked in the pitch blackness, as the scuffle with the entity had blown out all their candles. Narena frantically felt around on the ground, located one, and lit it as quickly as she could.

"Oh my Yew! Nyxen!" Sebillon gasped, and rushed to his slumped form. "Nyxen, can you hear me?"

Narena and Kellen hurried to Nyxen's side, and held up his head. "Nyxen, wake up!" Narena cried, unable to control the tears.

Nyxen shifted, and gulped. "I'm still here," he mumbled. He winced in pain each time he took in a breath.

"It looks like he has some broken bones," Kellen said. "I'm not sure if we should move him."

"This is all my fault!" Sebillon wailed, tears streaming from her eyes. "I should have just let that darkness destroy me!"

"Don't you dare say that," Nyxen muttered. "I'd do it again if I had the chance."

Sebillon gazed at Nyxen for a moment, then turned her eyes up to Narena and Kellen. "Go on, you two. I'll stay with him."

Narena and Kellen stared at the faery for a moment, and hesitated, looking helplessly from Nyxen to Sebillon, and back again.

"Did you hear me? I said GO! *NOW!*"

Narena hesitated. "But..."

Narena, you must go, Hawthorne's voice pierced in her thoughts again. *Now!*

"Take good care of him, Sebillon," Narena said. "Nyxen, stay strong. I love you, little brother."

"I love you too," Nyxen gulped. "Now, please go."

Sebillon nodded and motioned for them to leave. Narena and Kellen took deep breaths, and lit another candle as they walked off. They could hear Sebillon quietly sobbing amid Narena's own choked weeps, but as they walked inward the sound faded away.

"He's not going to die, is he?" Narena whispered to Kellen.

Kellen said nothing, but put his arm around Narena and held her close, providing as much comfort as he was able to in their current predicament as they trudged further on into the cave, and deeper into the darkness.

CHAPTER 21

The oxygen was thick, a feature of the dark part of the Forest immediately apparent to Felide. Disembodied screams and wails could be heard from all directions, though the warrior seemed not to notice them, as he was not one to be readily intimidated.

In his peripheral vision, Felide could make out swirls of red and blue swooping around, the blurs of color carrying nymphs wielding blades while being clutched within claws. Black, pulsating masses flew around, screaming and darting toward the soaring birds. Grotesque creatures, that were once beings or animals, writhed around on the ground, showing their distinct features of what they once were vaguely through their gruesomeness before engulfing themselves into blackness as entities and taking off in flight to the thick of the battle.

"Look out!" a cawing voice called, and Felide looked up to see a crow barely graze his forehead, slamming into an entity that was headed toward him.

"Thanks!" Felide managed to yell back, but the crow was gone and now another black mass was on its way in his direction.

Felide readied an arrow and released, slicing through the third eye and causing the entity to dissipate in a poof of black smoke. He turned around to find another coming toward him, and again he soared an arrow perfectly to take it down. He did this again, and again, but as fast as he could destroy one, more would keep coming, squeezing out of the earth as if summoned up from the underworld.

Time seemed to slow as Felide looked around at the battlefield through the sides of his eyes, battling entities simultaneously. The trolls had increased their presences, puffing up their bodies to appear much larger as they projected themselves off rocks and low hanging branches, blades in hand, stabbing blindly at the masses, hoping to land a strike between the eyes.

Arrows soared through the air, shot by faeries within the trees and nymphs from various vantage points among the branches, rocks, and fallen logs on the Forest floor. Foxes snarled and bore their canine teeth, snakes struck their teeth at the masses, even the rabbits and squirrels slashed their claws and struck with their incisors. Deer charged antlers first at the masses, and toads lay in wait, buried under dirt, snapping upwards at the masses who dared get close enough to their ambush. Perfect timing on these strikes was key, and the multi-species army was proving to be a promising band of warriors. But no matter how many times an entity would be cast out of the Forest, it seemed another was ready to take its place.

Please, he implored within his mind. Sator, Arepo. Watch over my son. Point him in the right direction. But who will protect us now that Labete is gone?

Felide could not shake away the pressing thoughts of Kellen. Even as he fought, his son's face kept peering into his mind. He thought of the time after his wife had passed away, and he had been stationed in Troll Kingdom for several months to ensure the kalpies weren't entering back into the Forest realm.

He was only seventeen. I never should have left him alone. Not when he needed me most.

Felide held off several entities as he made his way to a tall, jagged rock where he felt he could have a good shot for his arrows, but also be able to get up and down from the rock as quickly as he needed to. He climbed his way to the top of the rock faster than he ever imagined he could, stood atop the rock, and scanned every direction around him.

A thick, black mass with blood-red oval eyes met his glance and squinted in a gruesome grin. It shot backwards like a slingshot before propelling itself full force at Felide's crouching nymph body. But Felide was ready for the shot. He let loose an arrow into the mass, which grazed the third eye but sliced into the corner of the entity's left eye. The being howled, and gathering its good eye upon Felide, thrust itself back in his direction.

Felide countered with a stab to the left eye again, though he had been aiming for the right, hoping to blind the entity. The stab was enough to stop the mass for another moment, but as Felide reached into his arrow bag found it to be empty. He felt his face drain of color, but nevertheless readied his blade.

The entity laughed maniacally and lunged itself toward Felide once more. Felide stabbed at the mass, but missed his target and instead was slammed in the abdomen and thrown off the rock, slumping onto the ground. The mass hovered above him, laughing and taunting at the warrior nymph.

Oh no, please don't let this be it. Not without saying goodbye to Kellen.

"Stupid nymph. Your time is about to end," it roared, and as Felide reached for his blade, the entity swooped down and knocked it into a patch of thick, prickly blackberry bushes. "I've been waiting thousands of years to enact my revenge upon you beings of light. You will never defeat Labete. Let your death teach your beings to never challenge us again!"

Please! Not now! Not without telling my son I love him! I never had a chance to say goodbye to her, I cannot die until I've said it to him!

The entity howled as it shot itself down upon the ground where Felide lay helplessly, waiting for the blow and keeping his eyes fixated on the glowing red eyes as they traveled toward him. But despite the impending doom, he for some reason felt a thickness of warmth around his body, as if he were being wrapped in a blanket.

The entity grew closer, but suddenly and out of nowhere, Virgil leaped out of the blackberry bush, Felide's knife clutched in his teeth, and stabbed the entity square in the third eye. The entity howled one last time before bursting into flames and ash and absorbing into the dirt.

Felide looked up at Virgil, who had dropped the blade, panting, and smiled.

"Guess we're even now?" the warrior nymph joked at the fox, picking up his blade.

"You bet. But who was that woman?"

"What woman?"

"She was crouched over you. Real pretty, and glowing white." Felide felt tears well in his eyes. "That was my wife."

"She sure loves you a lot... to come back to protect you like that."

"I know."

Virgil tossed Felide his blade and crouched his shoulders. Felide climbed up and lifted his blade to the sky, hollering as Virgil galloped back into battle.

"For my son!"

CHAPTER 22

In his library, King Alston had nearly completed compiling all the necessary ingredients for his spell. He had located *The Forest Grimoire* and followed the instructions down to every minute detail. All that was left was to cast a circle of salt, burn the herbs, and recite the incantation.

"But it needs to be done outside," he trailed off under his breath.

"Anything I can help you with, darling?" Tiatana's voice rang in his mind. Alston looked up and found his wife standing in the doorway.

"No, no sweetheart. I've got everything under control."

"Have you?" A sweetness pinched with a hint of sarcasm was in her tone, but Alston was not one to notice anything beyond the inherent beauty of her form, and the sparkling blue eyes and shimmering golden hair that had enamored him for decades.

"I'm fine, dear. I need my privacy right now."

"For what? To perform your spell?"

"How do you know what I'm doing?"

Tiatana giggled. "Why, it's a wife's duty to know what's going on with her husband."

"You're so observant. Now, go see if Lyren will start some dinner for us. I'll be there after he rings the bell."

"Alston..."

He sighed exasperatedly. "Yes?"

"Have you seen Rowan? I mean, since he disappeared."

"No. Why?"

"Oh. Strange. Because I'm fairly sure I met him in a dream, and he said he's spoken with you."

"It was just a dream."

"Okay."

Alston watched as his wife turned her back to him, her long dress sweeping around in a wisp of air and disappearing from sight. He got up from his desk and gathered his ingredients.

"If it works, it works," he muttered to himself. "If it doesn't, well, I'll likely be killed with the rest of my kingdom and then there won't be a Forest anyway."

Alston made his way outside and to the courtyard, a breathtaking garden filled with shrubberies and all the wild roses and violets a royal nymph could desire. In the center of it all stood Alston himself, in statue form, mouth agape to spit water into the pool below his feet.

"In front of the fountain seems like a good place to do the spell," he chuckled. "Maybe doing it in front of myself will make it even more powerful!"

"I'm not sure if you ever had any power," a husky voice spoke from behind. Alston whipped around to look once again into the eyes of his son, who was perched upon the side of the fountain's pool. "And if you did, you certainly had no clue how to use it."

"Rowan! You've come back! You look more solid than the last time

I saw you. Are you alive?"

"Nope, sorry. Still dead. But I have some good news. All this hullabaloo that's been going on the Forest has weakened the barriers between our Forest realm and the spirit ones. Walking amongst the living has never been this easy, and it's only getting easier the more the falling progresses."

"How is that good news?"

"It's good because it means I can exist in this realm with you and Mother. It's like I never died."

"But you did die, Rowan, and nothing good can come of the realms intertwining."

"So, what then? You don't want me back? Is that how it is, Father?"

"It's not that. I've just always felt like spiritual realms were never anything to toy with."

"Then what do you think this is?" Rowan replied, motioning his hand toward the area where Alston intended to perform his spell. "You think this isn't toying with the spiritual world?"

"This is for the good of the Forest!"

"And now you suddenly care about the good of the Forest? When you almost single-handedly brought the bad into it in the first place? And you do know you need a sacrifice for this spell to even work properly, right?"

"Oh, I didn't know I needed one." Alston looked down at the book in front of him. "Ah, there it is. I suppose you're right."

"Sacrifice yourself."

Alston guffawed. "I don't think so. My kingdom needs me. It would need to be someone who's fairly useless."

"I'd say you're a good fit then!" Rowan laughed. "Don't worry

Father, I can take care of that. You just worry about finishing your little spell here. Leave the sacrifice to me."

Alston felt his face get hot. "Leave me then! I care not for your patronization. And stop bothering me while I'm clearly busy with matters of the living world. Either you're alive or dead. Do me a favor and choose one."

"I don't have a choice," Rowan growled. "And soon, neither will you." And with that, his image slowly faded away as it had done before.

Alston's mouth hung open as he stared at the spot where his son had once been. Not once, but twice now, Rowan had made his presence abundantly clear to his father, and Alston could not wrap his mind around the impracticality of the entire situation.

These daydreams will render me useless. There are more important things at hand.

Alston tried to flush it from his mind as he continued the spell where he had left off. He cast his circle of salt and blended the herbs in a quartz bowl. He then sat within the circle cross-legged, set the herbs aflame, and began to read the incantation aloud.

CHAPTER 23

 think we're almost there," Narena whispered to Kellen as they ventured further into the depths of the cave. "I can feel the evilness upon us."

"The thickness of the air makes it difficult to breathe," Kellen mumbled back.

"And the heat is getting more intense."

"Try to stay calm and focused. I'm right here with you."

"We're getting closer."

Labete is near, Narena, Hawthorne's voice spoke again in her mind. *Trust in yourself.*

The pair both stopped in their tracks, though the dim candlelight did not show anything ahead of them except a thick blackness that the two were now very acquainted with. Kellen shoved Narena behind him and squinted his forest-green eyes to see deeper into the infinite black hole that was before him. Narena closed her own eyes, and tried to mentally connect with Hawthorne again. But her mind was frazzled, and so many thoughts poured into her mind that she could not discern any message anymore, let alone one from her distant amphibious friend.

Narena pondered this strange reaction of hers, closing her eyes when something presented itself that was potentially unfavorable to her. Never had closing her eyes in a situation helped her, but she never seemed to learn that lesson.

Closing your eyes didn't help you with that toad entity, she scolded herself. It never helps you! And by doing this, you're just like Alston.

She recalled a time when she and Nyxen had been enjoying themselves as children, sliding on huge maple leaves down the patches of snow that cascaded down the rocks and fallen logs in the winter. One of these times she had not given Nyxen enough time to finish his descent down a particularly large hill, and had, in all her excitement, began sliding at rapid speed down the hill shortly after he began his slide. She knew she would hit him, as she raced down the hill at the mercy of gravity itself, but could not do anything herself to make her leaf stop. So she screamed his name and slammed her eyes shut just before the impact, which left Nyxen with a broken arm for quite some time.

Why would I possibly be shutting my eyes again at a time when I could actually use the added sense to make a quick decision? Narena thought, and opened her eyes as wide as she could and scanned the darkness in front of her.

"Kellen?" she whispered. Kellen found her hand and squeezed it. "Kellen, the shadows are moving."

"They're just shadows Narena... I smell something much more foul ahead of us."

Narena sniffed the air and she too smelled the awful odor emanating from just in front of where their little nymph bodies stood. It smelled like a rotting corpse, one that perhaps baked in the sun for several days, infested with flies laying disgusting eggs that would hatch into writhing, mucousing maggots. It was a smell similar too, though in no way less intense than Odila's corpse in the clearing, and oh! How Narena had wished that she would never experience that stench again in her lifetime!

The smell got worse, and Narena lifted the bottom of her tunic to cover her delicate button nose with.

"So I guess the divination was correct," a raspy, yet deep booming voice echoed in the cave walls from every direction around the pair. "Nymphs."

This voice had never been heard in such grotesqueness by either of the two, though they inherently knew exactly whose voice was speaking to them.

"And I hope you are ready to be destroyed by nymphs, Labete. Or should I say, Agrimon," Kellen said confidently.

Gruesome-shaped shadows danced around the walls of the cave that seemed to be closing in on them in the flickering candlelight, yet no form was visible to their eyes. The smell, however, was still very apparent, and as Labete spoke more, intensified.

"Little Narena and Kellen. I know all about you. I've been watching you for a long time in my mind's eye, waiting for you to finally push your tiny little existences enough to make it to my lair. It's too bad you have no more companions left to help you, though you can thank me for that, as I made sure of it myself. You think you can come in here and destroy me? You have no idea of the magnitude of what you're dealing with. I am not but one Higher Spirit, but *two*! Get ready to be sent back into the dirt where you belong!"

"You are the one who was sent to live in the dirt! The Higher Spirits cast you out, and you're just bitter! You will never destroy Nymph

Kingdom, and you will pay for what you've done to this Forest!" Narena screamed at Labete, with a fervency she had never felt before.

"Narena, Narena. You are foolish indeed. Tell me, where is your brother Nyxen? No need, actually, because I can tell you. Lying in the mud on the ground of a cave below us, taking in his very last breath. Don't believe me? See for yourself..."

Narena felt a sharp pain in her head and a force that closed her eyes immediately, and despite her attempts to reject the feeling, was shown a picture in her mind of her brother, laying right where she had left him, with Sebillon weeping over his limp body, begging him not to perish.

"I've read about this deception before. I know this is not the truth."

"But it is, my dear nymph, and I can prove it." Labete roared, and in a tornado of black-and-gray smoke Nyxen's body appeared and hovered in the dim light right in front of where Narena and Kellen stood, with Sebillon still clutching to him tightly as the incapacitated nymph and faery slammed onto the cave ground.

Nyxen groaned. "My head," he whispered. "My head is killing me."

"Don't think about it," Sebillon sobbed. "Think about happy times. Hold on, Nyxen. Please."

"I just keep seeing my parents," Nyxen muttered, as if he hadn't heard the faery. "Their death is replaying over and over in my mind. When they saved Alston. They... they jumped in front of him. Told him to hide. And he did. Like the coward that he is. He hid, and let them die fighting for his life."

"How can you see that? You said you were really young when it happened."

"The trees are showing me..."

"But Nyxen we haven't seen trees since the base of the mountain..."

Nyxen slumped onto Sebillon's lap, and the faery lifted her head to make eye contact with Narena, who stood, frozen, gazing back at her deteriorating brother.

"Believe me now?" Labete said.

Narena couldn't take it anymore. She fell to her knees before the blackness in front of her, and screamed.

"*WHY?* What happened to you, Labete? Why would you want to inflict so much pain upon beings who are so harmonious and good? I thought you were a Higher Spirit, one who is supposed to protect the Forest!"

"I was a Higher Spirit! Until I found the perfect balance with my Under Spirit counterpart, Agrimon. At first I didn't want him to possess me, but found upon our fusion that together, we could mold the Forest into what it's never been powerful enough to be!

"So I trained your King Alston as a king against the wishes of the other Higher Spirits. They said he wasn't mentally ready to be a king. They said he was too selfish, too vain. But I believed in him, taught him everything I knew, put my trust into him that he would be a great king. But then he became ignorant. Ignorant to the problems of the other kingdoms. Apathetic to the troubles of others. Concerned only with his image and perceptions of others as king. And we all know what happens when negative feelings like vanity, ignorance, and apathy combine in one's soul. It exacerbates one's ego and fills them with fear.

"Fear combined with the disgusting influence of the world beyond the Forest breed... no, seethe, negativity. And thus the darkness made its home inside of me. As my bitterness and thirst for revenge consumed me, I submitted to the darkness, and Agrimon and I have become one. But look at all it's gained me! I am now the most powerful Spirit of the

Forest!" Labete boomed laughter from all directions.

At the start of Labete's rant, Kellen noticed that a discernible form was beginning to manifest into focus in front of him. As Labete continued speaking and revealing more about himself, the form became more and more visible. It was extremely large, much larger than Kellen and even larger than a human witch. No eyes were yet visible, and Kellen wondered if there would be eyes to appear at all, since Labete was once a Higher Spirit and likely had few physical weaknesses, if any at all.

The form had resembled a large black blob at the start, but as Labete revealed more about the nature of his falling the blob morphed into a more humanoid form, though still giant in stature, and the features exaggerated—extremely long fingers, large ears, thick feet. No actual facial features were apparent, and still no eyes made an appearance on the form.

Kellen knew right then and there that he would probably only have one chance to get in a good shot at the third eye, and who even knew if hitting the eye would work. He could only estimate by the shape and size of the form, and where he saw the arms and the very top of the head of the form to be.

His mind raced back to the time he had just begun his warrior training, and had passionately drowned himself in his studies, striving to be the most knowledgeable warrior in addition to the most physically strong. He excelled in his studies, and eventually in every other test he had been presented with during his early trials. All the while he had been trying to make a name for himself, trying to make his superiors overlook the fact that he was the great General Felide's son, and prove that he could be a great warrior in his own right.

Kellen thought of all the times when superiors would roll their eyes at his test scores or after a physical trial, and whisper among themselves that Kellen's success was surely attributed to being a complete genetic copy of his father.

After so many such incidences, Kellen then decided to strive to be average. He had given up in a way, just resolved himself to wanting to not be noticed, and that even if he were to be a great warrior, he would never, ever, outshine his father Felide. He never felt the passion again that he felt when he first began his warrior training, even after he was given his own command.

Well, until now, that is. Until he saw Narena and fell so in love, so hard for her that every passion of hers became a passion of his own, radiating with the brightest light of love within his heart and soul. Narena's passion for life was infinite, and even in the darkest of times she had never given up hope. It was only now, as he looked at his love upon her knees, trying to choke her sobs for her murdered brother, that he saw her at her weakest. It was now that she needed his help the most.

Kellen wrought his mind of all the thoughts that were trying to force their way in, lost all sense of sanity, and pulled an arrow from his pack. Before even a second had passed the arrow was flying through the thick cave air, whirring the short distance straight through the head of Labete's form, right where a third eye would be located if Labete were a typical entity. But the arrow was futile, and Kellen heard it snap onto a rock wall in front of him. Labete laughed.

"O my great warrior, I cannot believe you do not know that only another Higher Spirit can destroy me. You must have ignored your studies," Labete taunted.

This comment infuriated Kellen, and though he tried to maintain his composure he felt an anger brewing within him. He clutched onto Narena, stood her up, and shoved her behind him. He puffed up his chest, broadened his shoulders, and looked straight into the black, pulsating, humanoid mass before him.

"Go ahead, Labete. Take me."

Kellen felt Narena dig her nails into his arms. "Are you crazy?" she hissed.

"I've never been more sane," Kellen turned to look at Narena. "And by the way, Narena," Kellen paused and turned to look right into Narena's orange eyes, which were twinkling in the dim candlelight. "I love you. I've always loved you."

Narena's eyes widened and filled with tears. "I love you too, Kellen," she whispered, and Kellen smiled in reply. He then turned back to face the former Higher Spirit who once protected him and his Forest.

"The Yew is being awakened as we speak, Labete. Soon you'll have to answer to him." He took a deep breath. "You can kill me, but you will *not* have Narena."

Chapter 24

Nessaba was just finishing her final incantation for awakening the Yew when even her utmost concentration could not provide ignorance to a shrieking sound that was getting closer and closer to the circle she was sitting within.

She tried to quickly finish her last, powerful words of the incantation when a gust of wind bearing the strength of a raging bull smashed into her side and knocked her clear out of her salt circle. Her arthritic body quivered, and as she tried to pick herself up off the ground another powerful blow sent her body flying into the side of a jagged rock, then slumped upon the ground once more. The witch felt something warm running down her face, and lifted her hand to feel that her hair was saturated in a thick, sticky liquid. Blood.

She wiped her forehead to prevent the blood from spilling into her eyes and lifted her head to see a black shadow with glowing red eyes perch itself atop the rock above and glare down upon her. It was an entity, for certain, but had very distinguishing features that entities do not typically bother to appear to beings of the Forest.

The entity was a writhing creature, with a long head and crab-like limbs which grew out of its bloated abdomen in segments, much like an arthropod of sorts. It had one enormous razor-sharp claw that it snapped in Nessaba's direction several times in a taunting manner.

"Show me what you once were, you coward!" Nessaba cried.

The entity laughed. "This is how I've always been. I've existed here long before this Forest, and will continue existing here long after it's destroyed."

Nessaba spoke in tongues back at the entity, trying to banish him away from her circle. And though under normal circumstances the incantation would have worked, it now seemed to have no effect on her adversary.

Nessaba felt her heart race. She knew she had to finish the spell, even at the mercy of being destroyed by this entity herself. She knew she could destroy it eventually, if she really battled it out, but feared that if she did not finish the spell in time that her little friends would surely perish at the hands of Labete. Nessaba, a human witch, had a very important choice to make that would wholly affect the outcome of this falling and every being that resided within this sacred Forest.

She looked up at the entity once more, who was baring its drool-dripped fangs back at her, snorting and panting for her soul.

In one swift movement, the witch pulled her body up and began dragging herself back toward the circle. The entity jumped down and scuttled quickly after her dragging body.

Nessaba reached into her pocket, pulled out a handful of strong-smelling dust, and threw it straight into the entity's face. The dust was ground up sage, which Nessaba always carried on her. It was known to keep entities at bay or to halt them temporarily, but the dust would not cast the entity away for good.

Sure enough, the dust seemed to stop the entity in its tracks for a brief moment, and Nessaba thanked the spirits mentally as she crawled back into the circle and spoke the final words of the incantation spell to awaken the Yew. Then she collapsed, gasping for breath, and feeling her body tingle as she lay in her salt circle losing more and more blood, and waited for the entity to gather its composure enough to return to finish her off.

At the very top of Lapis Mountain, a rumbling began that would have stirred a giant even in the furthest depths of slumber. The dirt within the peak of the mountain began to smolder, and a thick gray smoke billowed out of the very top. An opening, only about the size of a sunflower's head, withdrew itself from the rock and became a hole.

Out of the hole emerged a white light, glittered with shiny, golden specks that manifested itself into the shape of a crow, though at least ten times the size of an actual living crow. The white crow stretched itself in mid-air before diving its existence downward, and veering slightly to enter the cave that the group was currently battling within.

The grim walls lit up as the white crow soared its way through effortlessly toward the location to which it was summoned. It cawed loudly, so much so that the echo through the cave shook the entire mountain.

Chapter 25

Narena stood behind Kellen, trying to muffle her sobs as Labete loomed over him. She felt Kellen's body quiver slightly for a split second, then he righted himself and took a swing with his blade at Labete's third eye. But yet again, the blade swished right through, and Kellen found himself nearly toppling over from his own weight.

"Stupid nymph. You can't hurt me," Labete roared, and instantly shot his body through Kellen's, who shoved Narena out of the way, took the blow, and fell to the ground.

"I... can't..." Kellen muttered. "But the Yew can. Just... you... wait..."

Labete laughed, and a pair of large, menacing, yellow eyes appeared as if invisible eyelids had opened. "The Yew is not coming! Gorgon took care of that one himself." He glared daggers at the beings.

"The Yew is more powerful!" Narena couldn't help but yell. "He is the alpha of all you Higher Spirits! He will awaken, and he will get rid of you once and for all!"

Labete laughed again, and took another shot at Kellen as he lay on the ground, tackling him to the ground once more. Kellen grunted and pulled himself to a sitting position, then clutched his side and groaned.

Narena looked helplessly at Kellen, then back to Labete. "You're disgusting," she said, staring the Spirit straight in the eye. "And stupid. If you think that any evilness you can bestow upon us is more powerful than love."

Labete whizzed over to Narena and hovered right in her eye line, while still managing to tower over her tiny nymph body.

"Your love for this miscreant will only fuel my energy once you watch me destroy him."

Narena felt her face boil. Never in her life had she felt so much hatred for anything, let alone a Spirit she admired and worshiped. All her anger brewed into sadness, and in a fleeting moment found herself feeling sorry for Labete. Sorry that he had been influenced by the darkness, and sorrier that he had even allowed himself to be influenced. Gorgon was powerful, this was indeed true, but in order for Gorgon to have gained so much power, love had to counterbalance.

But it was Narena's love for Kellen that prompted her to stand against Labete, knowing full well that at any moment he could, and would, destroy her very existence. Kellen's life now hung by a thread, and Narena felt an energy well up inside of her. She quickly glanced from Kellen to her brother, then back to Labete.

Narena glared daggers into the once Higher Spirit. "You are weak," she said forcefully. "And you're only growing weaker. I, on the other hand, grow stronger as more and more love fills my heart. You will never succeed in making this Forest fall, even if you kill me right now, because there's too much love here for you to overpower.

"And if you, Labete, are now fused with Agrimon, shouldn't you cease to exist? You are nothing, because the day you turned away from love is the day you became nothing."

Labete wailed as he slammed through Narena's body, knocking her to the ground. Kellen screamed and tried to drag himself toward her, but Labete crashed into her again and knocked her far away from him.

"I feel sorry for you," Narena gasped. "I pity your very existence."

This comment seemed to infuriate Labete. His shadow outline fluctuated, and his eyes grew more intense. He pulled back slightly from Narena's front, and twirled his long, curling fingers to enact a swirling ball of hissing smoke that tickled between his fingers. The ball stunk of a gaseous odor, and Labete had no problem tossing it back and forth between his decrepit hands.

"When I'm done with you," he growled, "you're the one that will be pitied."

Labete pulled his arm back and released the gaseous ball in Narena's direction. This time, however, she did not slam her eyes shut but watched as it approached her. The ball soared closer and closer, and Narena could feel the wisps of smoke tickle the small hairs on her face. But the ball inexplicably stopped before hitting her, and hovered in front of her eyes before simply falling to the ground.

"What?! What is it doing?" Labete roared.

"She can't be killed," another voice from Labete's vicinity hissed. "It won't destroy her."

"Then what will?!" Labete boomed, and created another smoke ball. He threw it at Narena but again, the ball stopped mid-air and dropped to the ground. Labete was livid.

"She can't be destroyed!" the other voice cried.

"Listen to Agrimon!" Narena yelled. "Your evil is no match for my love!"

"Kill the other one, then!" Agrimon hissed.

"Then if I can't destroy you, I'll destroy him!" Labete wailed, and threw a smoke ball in Kellen's direction. It narrowly missed, but would have hit its target had Kellen not quickly rolled out of its way.

Labete formed another ball and drifted over to where Kellen was trying to crawl away. He loomed over him and cackled, readying his arm for another throw. Narena's eyes widened and she ran as fast as she had ever known her little legs to run toward the altercation.

Labete pulled his arm back, and thrust the smoke ball with the force of a hurricane toward Kellen. But before the ball connected, Narena leaped forth—eyes closed—in its path, halting it in its tracks and causing it to fall once more.

Narena hesitantly opened her eyes to find herself suddenly blinded by a bright white light, which seemed to radiate in gold and pulsate against the walls of the crevice.

"Shut your eyes!" Kellen shouted, to which Narena obliged.

Narena fumbled around on the ground, using any sense she could to try to locate Kellen in the midst of all the blinding white light. She felt his arms wrap around her body and clutched onto him tightly, her eyes darting around in her eyelids, trying desperately not to look directly into the light. She then noticed the light wane a bit through her eyelids and was able to open her eyes enough to make out a form in the shape of a large bird. It resembled a crow, but was white, very large, and glittered in gold specks.

"*That* is the Yew?" Kellen whispered.

"Of course it is, Kellen. He's perfect. He's beautiful!"

The Yew did not acknowledge the two nymphs, but rather kept his attention focused solely on the Labete-Agrimon hybrid. He stared deeply at it, almost as if he were bestowing some kind of forgiveness upon the being that had fallen into a pawn of Gorgon's diabolical scheme.

Then suddenly, without warning, the Yew opened its beak as widely as it could.

"Cover your ears!" Narena said to Kellen, and the two slapped their hands over their ears and ducked close together.

The Yew tilted its head back and resounded a booming caw.

CHAPTER 26

The caw had a vibration all its own, and embodied both ultra- and infra-sound that shook not only the mountain, but Narena and Kellen's insides as well. Labete wailed, and thrashed around as if in some form of immense pain.

"Get out of the way!" Kellen yelled, and fervently pushed Narena into the side of the cave wall, shielding her body with his own. Narena peeked her eyes out from under Kellen's arm and watched with wide eyes as the Yew continued its attack upon Labete.

With a swift swipe of the wing, the Yew swung at Labete, crashing into him and tossing him into the wall like a rag doll. Labete shot back, only to have the Yew tilt its body sideways to punch in another blow. But Labete came right back, and the Yew countered his attack with a forceful stab of its beak, causing Labete to roar in agony.

Narena gasped as she saw this weakened state of Labete. His aura was a sickly-looking smoky-gray and much smaller than it had been before. His large, yellow eyes were now stained with red, protruding veins, and as

Narena watched, the eyes found hers and glared right back, promising certain death if it were not for his current predicament.

But before Narena could be stared down any further, the Yew flew into Labete, causing the Spirit hybrid to scream a final wail. Labete promptly burst into flames, turned into ash, and absorbed, sizzling, into the ground. But the echo of the wail remained, and rang in Narena's ears.

Kellen's body loosened and Narena slipped out from under his arms. The two righted themselves and, upon realizing to whom they were in the presence of, fell to their knees and shielded their faces to the ground. But the Yew cawed softly, so the two slowly stood back up.

The Yew looked down at the small beings who stood before him, and seemed to smile in an odd sense. He leaned down to look face to face with Narena and Kellen.

"Thank you," Narena whispered with tears in her eyes. "I'm sorry for crying, I'm just sad that my brother's gone."

The Yew looked over to Nyxen and Sebillon. Then his eyes turned to Kellen.

The Yew reached out his right wing and lightly brushed Kellen's forehead in several quick, linear patterns. A bright white light, sprinkled in golden reflections radiated from his head in the shape of a symbol that Narena recalled having seen once before, in *The Forest Grimoire*.

"What's he doing?" Kellen's voice was shaky. "My brain is tingling!"

"It's the symbol of healing," Narena replied. "The Yew is blessing you!"

The Yew looked at Narena, nodded, and began to back away from Kellen. He then turned around and hopped away, in the direction of the entrance to the cave. As he got further and further away, the light emanating from his existence faded away, and in the split second that

Narena found herself mesmerized by the glow of the Yew, he was gone.

Narena fumbled around until she was able to light a candle, as the absence of the Yew caused the cave to once again welcome the little beings' victory with pitch blackness. Once it was lit, Narena and Kellen rushed to Nyxen's body and leaned over him, listening for a heartbeat.

"I'm pretty sure he's not completely gone yet," Sebillon spoke up. "He's pretty close, but I can feel the smallest heartbeat lingering on."

"Don't just stand there," Narena lightly tapped Kellen with the back of her hand. "You just were given the power of healing. Do something about this!"

"I'm not sure what to do," Kellen mumbled back.

"Lay your hands over him. One over his forehead, one over his chest. And concentrate!"

"You can do it, Kellen!" Sebillon cheered on, wiping the tears streaming from her eyes. "Bring Nyxen back!"

"Come on, Nyxen," Kellen muttered. "You can't go yet. Not after all this." He looked at Sebillon, and the look on her face shocked into his brain the memory of his father's expression when he had informed him of his mother's passing.

Kellen closed his eyes and thought hard about what he was intending to do. He took every ounce of fervency that had ever contributed to being a warrior, every emotion that he had ever locked away inside of him, and every morsel of love that had ever crossed his path. Then he thought of Narena, and felt a jolt of electricity shoot up his spine.

Nyxen's body began to glow with a bluish aura, and his previously muddled skin began to slowly fade into color. He gasped in a huge breath, then sat up, coughing.

"Nyxen!" the two girls screamed in unison.

"Welcome back, buddy," Kellen beamed.

"Am... am I alive?" Nyxen asked, his eyes darting around. "I felt so... at peace. But it's good to be back. And no headache anymore!"

"Can you walk?" Narena asked, and her brother lifted himself up and tried.

"I think I'm fine to walk."

"Good. Now, let's get out of here!" Kellen said, and began leading the way out of the cave.

After quite a long while of walking, the group finally made it to a point where some daylight was beginning to peer into the fading darkness. Narena ran ahead to the opening of the cave and fell to her knees, soaking up the sunlight as if she had not known the warmth of it before.

As the rest of the group caught up to her, Narena turned her head around and smiled. Kellen winked in reply.

"Now all we need is Hawthorne," Narena said. "I hope he's still where we left him."

The group trekked down the mountain's side, nearly tumbling down the rugged terrain as they descended. Sebillon could have had no trouble fluttering herself down on her own but insisted on staying close to Nyxen, who leaned on her for support.

"I'm so happy you're alive," Sebillon whispered in Nyxen's ear. "I almost lost you."

"What's it to you?" Nyxen joked. "I thought you might be happy to be rid of me."

Sebillon's eyes met his, and a slight twinkle shimmered in her iris. "If I wanted you gone, I'd have taken care of it myself! One arrow and you'd be toast!"

Nyxen laughed. "I love that I can see the mischief in your eye. I guess I was wrong about faeries. You folk are not so bad, after all." He paused. "Don't you have something to say about nymphs now?"

Sebillon stared at him blankly for a moment, then slowly began to speak.

"Up until today, I thought nymphs were among the lowest of Forest creatures. I thought they were dirt-walkers, bottom-feeders, useless, oblivious, and ignorant." She noticed Narena and Kellen had stopped in their tracks, and were listening intently as well. "But now I've seen that not only are nymphs courageous, but they are also selfless, kind, powerful, and very, very strong. Not only have I made friends on this journey, but I truly feel like I've found a family."

"Now do you intend on sharing these new found sentiments with your kingdom?" Kellen asked with a skeptical expression.

"I think I'm going to have to!" Sebillon replied, her eyes sparkling again.

"Why is that?" Narena asked.

"Well, the faeries are going to wonder why I have a nymph for a husband!" Sebillon giggled, and held Nyxen closer. Then her face switched to serious. "It might take awhile for the faeries to accept us as a couple. It's better if he comes to my kingdom."

Narena looked at her brother, her mouth agape. "Nyxen, when was this decided? Where was I?"

Nyxen hesitated. "Uh, it was after I got hurt. Sebillon lied over me and we talked quietly. About our feelings and such. For each other. That's right, I'm a flutterbum."

"Yeah," Sebillon broke in. "We decided that if we survived that, we'd get married."

Narena stared at Sebillon, then Nyxen, and softened her brow. "I can't think of a better girl for you. I wish you two all the best." She turned to the faery. "And I can't believe it! I'm going to have a sister!"

"Um, I hate to break up this love fest," Kellen said, peering down a ridge. "But I'm seeing... and smelling... something we may want to avoid."

"What is it?" Nyxen asked.

"Let's just go around this way," Kellen replied, leading the group in another direction, but still downwards. "Do not look down there! That's a direct order."

Narena pretended to follow Kellen's demands, but the second he turned his eyes away from her she dashed back toward the ridge and looked down to witness a sheer terror of sights.

Nessaba, the human witch, was laying perished in a circle of salt, her body twisted in a grotesque, unnatural position, with her legs contorted nearly all the way around her head. Her eyes were fixated in a cold, unfeeling glare, staring up at the sky as if begging for mercy. Flies buzzed in cylindrical patterns around her corpse, and a horrendous smell emanated up the mountain's side.

"Oh no," Narena gasped, and felt her stomach turn all the way up to the back of her throat.

"Hey, I told you not to look down there!" Kellen grabbed Narena by the arm and pulled her away from the horrible sight.

"What was it, Narena?" Sebillon asked.

"It... It was Nessaba," Narena said quietly. "She's dead. Someone, or something, killed her while she was doing the spell."

"Or after," Sebillon said. "Because the Yew came."

"You're right," Narena said. "It had to have been after."

"I seem to remember something about a sacrifice," Nyxen chimed in. "Didn't the Elder Triage say we'd need one?"

"I guess she was it," Sebillon said.

"She sacrificed herself for us," Narena said. "We owe her our lives."

"Hey, I think Hawthorne's spot is just down this ridge," Kellen broke in. "Come on, let's see if he's still there."

The group made its way down a few jagged rocks, reaching the point where Hawthorne had stayed behind. Narena rushed to the area and began frantically calling out for her salamander friend.

"Hawthorne! Hawthorne!"

"He's not here," Kellen said.

"He has to be!" Narena cried. "Hawthorne! Hawthorne! Where are you?!"

Narena searched under rocks and in piles of dried leaves until she finally reached a smooth, oval-shaped rock that had a massive amount of moss packed underneath it. She tore through the moss to reveal a curled-up ball of moist, pulsating, leathery skin, and poked it.

"Hawthorne?" she asked quietly.

The ball stirred, and suddenly Narena's finger felt hot to the touch. She tore her finger away just in time to see the ball engulf in a beautiful dance of red, orange, yellow, and blue flames. The ball uncurled, and the smiling amphibian face of Hawthorne emerged.

Narena shrieked in delight, and as the flames surrounding Hawthorne's body faded away, the small, orange-eyed nymph ran to her friend and hugged him so tightly it nearly knocked the wind straight out of his tiny, salamander body.

"Are you all okay?" Hawthorne asked once Narena had released her grip on him. "I spent this whole time meditating, and I got the distinct feeling that at least one of you was dead! And since I don't see Nessaba with you, I have to assume the worst."

Narena hung her head, and Hawthorne nodded solemnly.

"Well, the sacrifice was certainly necessary," Hawthorne said. "How kind of her to do that for us."

"She truly was an amazing witch," Narena replied softly.

"Enough chit-chat," Kellen spoke up. "I mean, we should probably get going. I don't know about you guys, but I'm ready to get home. I'm sure we can discuss all this along the way."

The group agreed and started walking back toward Nymph Kingdom, but Nyxen wasted no time in questioning Hawthorne of his visions during the battle with Labete.

"I kept seeing my parents sacrifice themselves for Alston over and over in my mind," he said. "And I knew it was the trees that were showing it to me, but couldn't figure out why they would do that. Or how, since the trees were far away."

"They were most likely acting through Sebillon," Hawthorne pointed out. "Faeries are arboreal elementals. They have a special connection with the trees, and I've certainly heard of them being used as catalysts like that before. I'm not sure why they showed you that either, but I can say that it was to your benefit. It helped you survive, so maybe it's best not to question why. Just be grateful for it."

"Would have been nice to not have a headache when the rest of my body ached too, but oh well. Thanks, trees!" Nyxen declared.

"The headache I can explain. It kept the blood flowing to your brain during your time of peril. Those headaches that you despise so much actually may have helped save your life," Hawthorne said.

"I never thought I'd say this, but I'm thankful for those headaches then."

"I'm thankful for them too," Narena beamed at her brother. "I don't know what I'd have done if I lost you, my favorite person to talk to."

"Speaking of talking, I must ask this of you," Hawthorne turned to address Narena. "And please know that I in no way take pleasure in asking you to relive the terrifying moments that just occurred, but in all my meditation some visions did not appear as clear as I would have liked. But I must ask, did Labete speak to you? Out loud, I mean."

"Yes, he did," Narena replied. "Why, is that bad?"

"For a Higher Spirit, yes. They're supposed to love, guide, protect, or direct us. None of which requires words of any kind. Speaking to you, and for as long as he did, most likely weakened him and only led him further to his demise. And it was very brave, and very important for you to speak with him for awhile, as it not only weakened him but bought you more time for the Yew to arrive. Very well done indeed."

"So I guess my stubbornness finally paid off!" Kellen chuckled, and clutched his arm tightly around Narena's waist.

"Wow," Narena replied. "I've never read anything like that before in any books."

"That's because it's ancient wisdom. The kind you get from being a sage. Some information is purposefully left out of books, because it's better not known."

"Interesting. Then you might know why Labete's fumes were futile against me."

"What?! How do you mean?"

"He kept trying to throw these horrible, stinking smoke balls at me. But each time one was about to hit me, it would stop right in its tracks. For no reason!"

"I don't think it was for no reason," Hawthorne beamed. "I think you have that something special inside you. Something every warrior wishes he had. And your father is the only normal being that I've ever come across with this particular gift. Besides you, now, that is. Guess it passed down," he said, chuckling.

"What is it?"

"Narena, your mind is so powerful and pure that if you think it hard enough, you can create a protective barrier around yourself, much like I did in the darkest part of the Forest. This is an ability that only sages and other blessed beings are able to do. Did you know you could do this?"

"No! I had no idea!" Narena could hear the frustration in her own voice. "So I could have put one around all of us in that cave, even my brother?"

"Don't beat yourself up about it," Kellen broke in. "How could you have known?"

"Everything happens as it should," Hawthorne said. "But one more question for you, Narena, because this is the only aspect left of today's events that I am still not entirely clear on—who performed the second spell to awake the Yew?"

CHAPTER 27

"S-second spell?" Narena asked. "It certainly wasn't any of us, unless Sebillon perfomed one while we were facing Labete."

"It was not me," Sebillon replied bluntly.

"She would need to have made a sacrifice anyway," Nyxen said. "And I was with her the whole time. It wasn't her."

"Then who was it?" Kellen asked. "I mean, if you think about it, couldn't it have been anyone in the Forest?"

"Not necessarily," Hawthorne replied. "It needed to be someone who wields some element of power. Whether by birth or appointed."

"The Faery King, maybe?" Narena said.

"I doubt it," Sebillon replied. "Faeries are not inclined to make sacrifices."

"Hmm, then I guess we may never know," Hawthorne said. "Which is too bad, because we owe whoever it was our thanks. It was that second spell that secured Labete's demise."

"Why is that?" Narena asked.

"Well, without the second spell the Yew could not have destroyed both Labete and Agrimon at the same time. If there had only been one spell, it's possible that the Yew would have destroyed Agrimon alone, and that would leave Labete to return to his status as a Higher Spirit."

"Why is that bad?" Nyxen said. "Don't we want him back to protect the Forest?"

"No," Hawthorne replied. "He was influenced in a negative way, and the darkness completely overtook him. I'm sure we'd be hearing from him again in future generations if he had not been destroyed, and I doubt his return would be in a positive mindset."

"It's probably for the best," Narena said. "The Forest is balanced again if both Labete and Agrimon were destroyed. And if it were that easy for Labete to turn bad in the first place, I'm not sure if we want him protecting our Forest."

"And with little beings like yourselves," Hawthorne chuckled, "I think the Forest is well-protected now anyway."

Narena pondered the conversation as the group walked back toward Nymph Kingdom, absorbing all the knowledge she had accrued in the last few days. But as they grew closer and closer to their home, she began to notice Hawthorne moving slower and slower, often falling behind the group and struggling to catch his breath. When the group reached where Salamander Kingdom once was, he stopped completely.

"Hawthorne, are you all right?" Narena finally asked, hanging back to support her salamander friend. "Do you need any help?"

Hawthorne took a breath. "No, I think you've done a lot to help recently! I'll be okay."

"Are you sure?"

"Well, I'm afraid I may need to be left behind."

"What?! Why?!"

"I can feel myself growing weaker by the moment. I don't think I'll last much longer."

"What do you mean?"

"I'm at the end of my life, Narena. And now I feel that my work here is done. I've avenged my kind and it's time for me to move on."

"No!" Narena cried. "You can't leave me!"

"I have to," Hawthorne whispered. "But I want to leave you with a parting gift."

"A gift? Your gift can be to stay! I need you!"

"You don't need me anymore. And since my kind were wiped out, you're going to be my only successor to my sage abilities. I'm going to give you the gift of seer sight. Come closer."

Hawthorne stood face to face with Narena and placed his slimy hand on her forehead, right between and slightly above her teary, orange eyes. Then he closed his own.

In an instant, Narena felt an energy swoop over her body, and she noticed a swirling mist encircle her and Hawthorne. She closed her eyes, and felt the energy flow through her veins. Then she experienced a shock, one so powerful that it threw her backwards, and as she hit the ground, she opened her eyes to see Hawthorne lying on the Forest floor in front of her.

"No!" she wailed. "Hawthorne!"

But the salamander did not reply, and instead laid motionless on the ground.

"What happened?" Kellen's voice demanded, and Narena noticed that he, Nyxen and Sebillon were standing over her.

"Hawthorne's gone," she whispered. "He's dead."

"What? How did this happen?" Nyxen said.

"He said it was his time. But he gave me his sage powers."

"I can't believe it. I thought he would just live out the rest of his life with us, at home. I guess he was pretty old as far as salamanders go."

"But still," Narena said, "it doesn't make it any easier."

"I'm sorry Narena," Kellen whispered as he embraced her.

"I'm sorry too," Sebillon chimed in. "He was a good being."

Narena nodded, her eyes swelled with tears. "Let's move him to a better resting spot."

The other three agreed and helped Narena move Hawthorne's body further into Salamander Kingdom.

"Here, I think this is his old house," Narena said when they had reached an old, rotting log that was covered in moss and fallen leaves. "I haven't been here in years, but I vaguely remember coming here as a child."

"I'm sure you're right," Kellen said. "Let's put him in here."

The group delicately placed Hawthorne's body under the log, then gathered together to speak a final blessing for their dead friend before they moved on.

"I just can't believe that he's gone," Narena said after they had gotten some distance away from Salamander Kingdom. "It's just, I've known him my whole life. We used to always gallivant around the Forest together. Looking for bugs and stuff."

"I'm going to miss him too," Nyxen chimed in. "I remember when we were little, if Mother ever couldn't find you, she'd have Father go search the area by the creek. They'd usually find you guys splashing around in the water or getting covered in mud."

"I remember you two always getting into trouble," Kellen piped up. "That's why I'd spy on you, to make sure you weren't getting yourself into something you couldn't get out of."

"Suuuure, that's why," Nyxen teased. "You were always sticking your big nose into Narena's business, with or without Hawthorne involved. I figured you had a thing for her even before our teenage years."

"Well it paid off, didn't it?" Kellen shot back with a big grin. "And I'm sure that Hawthorne would be ecstatic if he knew what I'm about to do next…" He stopped and turned to face Narena, halting her and holding both her hands.

"Narena, I know we've known each other a long time, and though we haven't always gotten along, it doesn't change how I've always felt about you. Every time I learn something new about you it's like I'm meeting you for the first time. Life with you would never be boring, that's for sure, and I can only be so lucky as to even play a small part in your existence…." he paused, "but that's not good enough. Narena, will you marry me?" He got down on one knee.

Narena's orange eyes grew wide and filled with a fresh set of tears, though this time they were not for the loss of her friend, but the excitement and love of a new beginning.

"Yes!" she cried, pulling Kellen up to his feet and shoving her lips on his, holding him close and feeling every muscle in his arms clasp tightly around her. "Of course I'll marry you Kellen! I've always loved you too!"

"Hurray!" Sebillon cheered, and Nyxen went over to Kellen and shook his hand.

"I couldn't have asked for a better brother," Nyxen grinned.

"Me too," Kellen replied. "And now that we are all betrothed, I think it's time for us all to go home."

"Yeah, let's hope there's a home to go back to!" Narena said, half-jokingly.

So the group headed off again toward Nymph Kingdom, the two couples walking hand in hand. Narena peered up at the sky, and saw that the sun was slowly but surely setting itself to bed. She hoped they'd reach home before dusk.

Chapter 28

Felide stood in confusion atop Virgil's neck as he scanned the darkest part of the Forest. The part of the Forest where, just moments ago, he and his army had been waging a full on battle against the dark entities sent by Labete to complete the falling of the Forest. What had been a living, breathing, scene of war before him just moments prior had suddenly, out of nowhere, come to a halt.

The dark entities which had been littering the trees and sky with their blackened smoke no longer flew about, and only a few small fires in mid-air could be seen around the warrior's eye line. The sun shone above, and even found its way into the dark sector of the Forest, where Felide could now make out something that appeared to be raining from the trees, and as he looked closer he found the rain to be a massive amount of dark gray ash cascading from the sky. The ash fell very slowly to the ground and made a slight wailing sound, as if whispering its final words to the Forest before absorbing into the dirt. When all the ash had fallen, Felide found it safe to call to what was left of his army.

"The entities are gone! Labete has been defeated!" he shouted. The army returned the fervor with a collective cheer.

"The ash is what remains of our fallen adversaries!" Virgil yelled. "Good prevails once again!"

"Congratulations everyone, we made it!" Felide announced. "You've all done very well for our Forest. Now, let's all go home!" The crowd hooted and hollered happily in reply.

Felide climbed atop Virgil's neck once more, and with the small amount of energy he had left, patted his fox friend and scratched the scruff of his neck, conveying to Virgil that it was indeed time to leave the dark part of the Forest and begin making their way back to Nymph Kingdom. Back home. He breathed an exasperated sigh of relief as Virgil took off, with the remaining members of the Forest army trailing behind.

Felide found himself finally able to relax once he and his army had ventured out of the darkest part of the Forest. He thought about what might be waiting for him in Nymph Kingdom, and whether he would even have a kingdom to return to.

If the dark entities are gone, either been destroyed or left to sink back into the dark holes they emerged from, that means Labete had to have been destroyed. He sighed.

But who awoke the Yew, he wondered. And who, if anybody, had the honor of looking upon him?

Felide had always wanted to be in the presence of a Higher Spirit, for it was well-desired among the beings of the Forest. Seeing a Higher Spirit was like looking at a stronger, more powerful, and overall more positive likeness of oneself, and Felide, as a warrior, had always longed to have a taste of such an energy.

He then wondered about his son, Kellen.

Had he survived the falling?

Felide quickened Virgil's pace, not taking into consideration the pace of the army that followed behind him. Nothing else mattered anymore, he needed to find out what happened to Kellen.

Narena, Kellen, Nyxen, and Sebillon were still on their way back to Nymph Kingdom when Kellen suddenly yelled for everyone to stop.

"What is it?" Narena asked.

"Just hang on a second, I hear something big coming our way."

The group ducked behind a bush and Kellen readied an arrow. The sound of galloping grew closer and closer, and Narena was able to see a blur of red stampeding down the deer trail they had been following.

"It's a fox," she whispered. "Kellen, it's a fox!"

"I see that," he replied. "But is it a good fox?"

"There's a nymph riding it!"

Kellen jumped out from behind the bush. "Hold it!"

Virgil skidded to a stop and turned quickly, his mouth agape with his tongue hanging out. He sniffed loudly as he bounded over to Kellen.

"Father?" Kellen asked, looking up at the nymph sitting atop the fox's back. "Father, is that you?"

"My son!" Felide replied, grinning from ear to ear. "I was rushing home to see if you were there! Are you all right?"

"I'm fine. I have my friends with me."

Narena, Nyxen, and Sebillon slowly emerged from behind the bush.

"Hi Felide," Narena said. "It's nice to see you."

"Same to you, little lady," Felide replied. "Nyxen! Good to see you too!"

"Same," Nyxen replied. "This is Sebillon."

"Hello there."

"Hi," Sebillon said meekly. "I've heard a lot about you."

Felide looked at Kellen. "Good things, I hope."

"Of course," Sebillon replied. "Only good."

"Father, where were you?" Kellen asked.

"Waging war in the darkest part of the Forest. By King Alston's order. Where were you?"

"Fighting Labete. Holding him off long enough for a human witch to awaken the Yew and destroy him. He's gone, Father. We killed him. The Forest is back in balance."

"You don't say," Felide said, rubbing his chin. "Well, son..." He paused for a moment, as Kellen waited in agony. "I couldn't be prouder of you. You are a true warrior."

Kellen couldn't help but allow a smile to curl around his face. "Thanks, Father."

"Now, why don't all of you climb on Virgil's back? You look tired and I bet you'd like a ride home." Felide grinned, and Virgil nodded in agreement.

The four climbed on the fox's back and they all rode off, following the deer trail that would surely lead them back to Nymph Kingdom, and much faster than was previously anticipated.

"Hey, Father," Kellen whispered over Felide's shoulder shortly after they were on their way.

"Yes?"

"I have something to tell you."

"What is it, my son?"

"I'm engaged to be married."

"To Narena?"

"Yeah, how'd you know?"

Felide chuckled. "I've always known, son. And I have to say, it's about time!"

Kellen laughed. "All right, all right. I guess I thought I was less transparent than I actually am."

"The beings that love you will always be able to read you," Felide replied. "Whether you like it or not."

"I'm starting to like it now."

"That's good. You're growing up. Another thing it's about time for!"

"Ha ha, very funny."

"Seriously, though, I couldn't be happier for you two. I really like Narena. Always have. And I think she's perfect for you."

"I think so too."

"Hey, didn't there used to be that sage salamander with you? What happened to him?"

"He passed away while we were walking back."

"That's unfortunate. He was a pretty powerful elemental. I used to have run-ins with his father every now and then."

"Yeah," Kellen trailed off, as his attention was now brought to a slight gleam in the near distance, shimmering from the moonlight into his green eyes. He breathed a sigh of relief, and slid over slightly to grasp his future wife as she cried out at the most beautiful of sights.

"We're home!"

Chapter 29

Virgil strode triumphantly through the threshold of Nymph Kingdom, as Narena, Nyxen, and Sebillon cheered.

"Where to?" he asked, cocking his head backwards slightly to look at Felide out of the corner of his eye.

"The palace, if you please. Straight ahead, you can't miss it."

"Do you mind if Sebillon and I get off?" Nyxen asked. "I need to start packing for my move to Faery Kingdom."

"Sure thing," Virgil replied, and leaned down so the two could disembark.

"I'll be there in a little bit," Narena called to her brother. "I need to take care of something at the palace first."

"Please bid Alston my goodbyes," Nyxen replied. "I don't think I'll make it over there before I leave."

"Okay, I will. See you soon."

Nyxen and Sebillon walked off, and Virgil trotted to the palace and went in. Narena, Kellen, and Felide climbed down from the fox's back after they reached the foyer.

"Where do you need to go, Narena?" Felide asked.

"To the throne room," Narena said. "To talk to Alston."

"Then we'll all go together."

The three nymphs and fox entered the throne room, where Alston sat with Tiatana by his side, much in a similar fashion to how the little beings viewed him just a few days ago. However this time, Lyren was nowhere to be seen.

"Ah, I see you've returned," Alston said as the beings righted their postures to stand in his presence. "Are you the only survivors?"

"Many other nymphs, faeries, trolls, and animals of the Forest returned to their homes after Labete was destroyed," Felide spoke up. "We suffered some casualties, yes, but we won the war against the darkness, your Highness."

"And what of your brother, Narena?"

"Nyxen is alive, but he's at home with his faery girlfriend," Narena said, tilting her head slightly.

"Faery girlfriend?! This falling shook up the structure of the Forest indeed. I certainly wouldn't have taken your brother to be a flutterbum."

"With all due respect, Sir, we've been through a lot the last couple days. We just wanted to let you know we were all okay," Kellen broke in.

"And we're all flutterbums now!" Narena cried. "There's no more need for all this hatred in the Forest! Can't you see that now? It only weakens us to something worse!"

Alston huffed. "I'm aware of this. And rest assured, no falling will ever so much as brush past our Forest ever again. Not on my watch."

"'Twas wise indeed to start that war," Felide said. "The Forest is most grateful to you."

"But they'd still be fighting that war if we hadn't awoken the Yew and held off Labete as long as we did," Kellen muttered under his breath.

"What was that, Kellen?" the king asked.

"Nothing," Kellen replied.

"Well I guess then…"

"No, wait a second here," Kellen broke in, furrowing his brow. "It's not nothing. Labete told us all about you, your Highness."

"And what did my teacher have to say?"

"He said that his decision to back you as king is what excommunicated him, and he also said that your ignorance helped him destroy other species."

"Did he also tell you that he was possessed, or did he manage to leave that part out?"

"We knew he was possessed," Kellen said, "but he also knew he was being possessed and did nothing to stop it. He embraced evil."

"Well I can't be expected to take to full responsibility for Labete's demise, nor for the falling."

"The faeries are right about you."

"And just how many beings' demises would it take for you to take responsibility for, let's say, anything?" Narena piped up. "Wasn't your son enough?"

"Young lady," Alston replied through clenched teeth. "You'd do best not to mention him in such context. I have half a mind to throw you, and your boyfriend here, out of Nymph Kingdom. Go live with the faeries, if you desire to share in their worthless opinions."

"But Alston," Narena replied, holding back tears. "I have much love for your son. As I do for every being that sacrificed themselves for the good of the Forest. Like Hawthorne and his species, or Nessaba, the human witch. And we ended the falling! We woke the Yew!"

"I'm afraid you are gravely mistaken," Alston said angrily. "Because it was I who awakened the Yew."

Narena stared at Alston in pure disbelief. She had momentarily forgotten about the second spell. She had thought for sure that it had been performed by one of the witches in the Elder Triage, but never had it crossed her mind that it could have been Alston. Narena had resolved herself to that thought, but as she processed the information her mind came back into focus.

"So it was you. Well, I certainly owe you an apology then," Narena said. "Your spell restored balance in the Forest. Nessaba's spell prompted the Yew to destroy Agrimon, and Labete could have continued his reign of terror had you not performed your spell as well."

"But wait," Kellen broke in, "Nessaba gave her life as a sacrifice for the spell, and that's what made it work. Who did you sacrifice?"

Alston fidgeted in his throne. "I didn't need one," he said forcefully. "My power is enough on its own."

Narena scrunched her eyebrows. It didn't sound right to her. But she shrugged at Kellen anyway and motioned to him that she was ready to go.

"Well, your Highness, Narena and I are really quite tired and should be getting home," Kellen announced.

"Very well," the king replied. "You are free to go. Felide, you stay. I'd like to discuss the war with you for a bit, if you don't mind."

"Yes, my king," Felide said.

Narena and Kellen bowed to the king and queen, then made their way out of the palace and back to Narena's oak tree home. There, they enjoyed a feast of human-sized proportions and then proceeded to sleep for three days straight.

When they all finally awoke, Nyxen and Sebillon packed up their things and bid their goodbyes to Narena and Kellen before leaving for Faery Kingdom. Shortly after they left, Kellen went to his old house, packed up what little belongings he had and moved in with Narena.

Many years passed since the falling and the balance of the Forest had been fully restored to its original harmony. Kingdoms were rebuilt and extant species repopulated, while new trees sprouted and winter rains washed away any trace of the falling into the earth.

Narena and Kellen have been married for some time, and Narena enjoyed a blissful pregnancy through the winter and spring months. But just days after spring turned to summer, she gave birth to a dark haired, orange-eyed son to whom the name Felix Hawthorne was given.

Nearly two decades went by, and Felix grew into a young warrior, following the tradition of the other members of his family. Happiness and harmony flourished, and the Forest had near forgotten the tribulations of their elders, the falling, and Labete. Though Felix certainly was no stranger to it, as he, even in his young adulthood, still frequently begged his parents to tell him their tales of their experiences that were on the way to becoming legends.

Felix so longingly wished to experience all the adventures of his parents, and whether it be that reason or perhaps an inherited desire of mischief, he enrolled to post at a warrior station in another kingdom of King Alston's choosing. Felix hoped for adventure, and to make a separation from living in his parents' shadows. And because of who he was, wasn't adventure imminent?

CHAPTER 30

King Alston had aged much in two decades, as he sat upon his throne, alone in the throne room, and wore his exasperation with life upon his face. He knew that the time would soon come for the Higher Spirits to begin deliberations on their new selection for Nymph King.

If Rowan were alive, he thought, he would be readying to take the throne at this time.

Alston sighed as he remembered his only son. He had wished for the kingdom to remain in the family, but alas, since he no longer had any offspring, it would be up to the Higher Spirits to decide.

King Alston got up from his throne and walked out into the foyer. The palace had changed much in the time that had passed, with less glitter and sparkle, and more stones that emitted good energy and absorbed any bad, such as limestone and quartz. The colorful gems that had once been scattered around the walls of the palace were much less, as most had been divided amongst the remaining kingdoms that had survived the falling, as a peace offering for prevention of a forced abdication.

Alston entered his quarters, and to his surprise saw that someone appeared to be sitting in one of his armchairs, facing out the window that looked out onto Nymph Kingdom.

"Hello?" the king called out, but received no reply.

Who could it possibly be? Maybe Lyren? But he disappeared two decades ago! It's simply not possible! But what if it is? Stranger things have happened. Yes, it must be Lyren. He's returned to me after all these years. But why won't he answer me? Perhaps he's sleeping.

He moved closer, and listened for the sound of someone breathing. None.

"Lyren? Is that you?" Alston said, standing a fox tail's length behind the chair. "Have... have you come back? It's been years, where have you been?"

No response.

Alston stepped closer, and slowly made his way around the side of the chair. He peeked around and quickly started to gag.

Lyren was slumped in the chair, obviously perished, with his face blackened with ash and frozen in a twisted death stare. His body was rotted, and yet in a way perfectly preserved, with the skin draped tightly over his skeleton, devoid of any living fluids. Alston covered his mouth with his robe to prevent himself from gagging, and stepped back from the chair in horror.

It's almost like... he's mummified. But how? And why?

"Hello Father."

The gruff voice resonated in Alston's skull, and he did not need to turn around to know who it was that stood behind him.

"Hello, Rowan," Alston mumbled as he turned around to face his son. "It's been awhile since we last saw each other, hasn't it?"

Rowan nodded. He looked as solid as the day he disappeared, blond hair, blue eyes, and scowled expression. But his hair no longer held the luster it once had, and his eyes lacked a sense of vitality behind them. But though his features were still prominent and his form solid as a living being, his aura did not radiate in the way that a living nymph's would. His skin was dull, gray, and muddy, his eyes were sunken, and his golden hair was stiff and dry.

Alston got a sense, as he looked his son up and down, that Rowan was slowly rotting away. His energy was not strong, and he looked at though he had crawled and clawed his way back up out of some kind of torturous underworld.

He's dead. Been dead for quite some time now. This is just another vision of him, even though he looks differently than he did before. Alston thought for a moment and carefully picked his words.

"Rowan, I know you are not the son I once knew, and you have no doubt escaped from some kind of terrible predicament in your afterlife that you can not be reborn in life's evolution, but I must beg of you... Why would you kill my dearest subject?"

Rowan took a step closer. "Don't you remember? A sacrifice was needed to awaken the Yew."

"And that's why he's been missing all these years?"

"Of course, where did you think he went?" He took another step toward the king.

"I wasn't sure, but I didn't think he was dead."

"Did you even try to find out what happened to him?" Another step.

"I had some subjects search around for a while, but they didn't find anything."

"How typical of you. You give your chancellor and your son the same treatment." He crept even closer.

"Why would you bring me this? What's your intention of showing me this corpse?"

"Simple, Father. I am here to eliminate any obstacle to the path of my destiny." Rowan was less than a fox tail's length away.

"And what destiny is that, Rowan? What are you here for?"

Rowan narrowed his eyes as he stepped directly into his father's eye line. "Exactly what I am entitled to, Father. I'm here to take my crown."

About the Author

T. Damon has always harbored an immense passion for not only writing, but animals and nature. Her added interest in all things magical and mythical inspired the creation of The Forest Spirit series, which embodies a little bit of everything she loves. When she's not writing, she enjoys spending time with her husband, daughter, and pets at her home in the enchanted forests of Northern California.

Other Works by the Author

Writing *As* T. Damon

The Haunting: Book 2 of The Forest Spirit series

The Reckoning: Book 3 of The Forest Spirit series

The Awakening: Book 4 of The Forest Spirit series
(Coming soon!)

Perchance to Dream:
"The Desperate Warrior and the Beast Who Walks Without Sound"
(Also available as a stand-alone paperback)

Writing *As* K.L. Teal

A Girl Named Dracula

Anthropoidea

9 781946 202338